He still had th[e]
breath away

It wasn't fair, Elizabeth thought fleetingly. It wasn't fair that after everything they'd been through, after all the grief and hurt and bitterness of the past eighteen months, he still had the power to take her breath away.

"Elizabeth! What are you—what brings you by here?"

He chose his words carefully around her, for so long, she wondered if either of them even knew how to relax anymore.

Coming over to stand behind his desk, his gray eyes raked her curiously. And no wonder. She hadn't been in his office in over a year. Not since before the accident.

"I decided to drop by and see if you have dinner plans."

He lifted a brow as he regarded her across the expanse of the desk. For the longest moment he said nothing and Elizabeth rushed to explain. "There's…something I need to talk to you about."

"I see." His gaze flickered, but she didn't have a clue what he was thinking. He seemed so remote, so cold. Nothing at all like the man who had barely let her out of bed on their honeymoon.

She didn't want to remember their honeymoon now. Or the night they'd made their precious son…. She couldn't do what she had to….

THE EDGE OF ETERNITY
AMANDA STEVENS

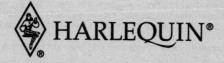

HARLEQUIN®

TORONTO • NEW YORK • LONDON
AMSTERDAM • PARIS • SYDNEY • HAMBURG
STOCKHOLM • ATHENS • TOKYO • MILAN • MADRID
PRAGUE • WARSAW • BUDAPEST • AUCKLAND

ISBN 0-373-22882-1

THE EDGE OF ETERNITY

ABOUT THE AUTHOR

Amanda Stevens is the bestselling author of over thirty novels of romantic suspense. In addition to being a Romance Writers of America RITA® Award finalist, she is also the recipient of awards in Career Achievement in Romantic/Mystery and Career Achievement in Romantic/Suspense from *Romantic Times* magazine. She currently resides in Texas. To find out more about past, present and future projects, please visit her Web site at www.amandastevens.com.

Books by Amanda Stevens

CAST OF CHARACTERS

Elizabeth Blackstone—Haunted by her son's death, she becomes vulnerable to an evil seduction. The only one who can save her is the man she turned away from.

Paul Blackstone—A weekend trip to save his marriage becomes a battle to save his wife's soul.

Roland Latimer—Is he a ghost trapped in the mists of Fernhaven...or a figment of Elizabeth's imagination?

Frankie Novak—Elizabeth's business partner has secrets of her own she must hide.

Nina Wilson—A woman who insists that she and Paul are meant to be together.

Dr. Julian Summers—Has he formed an unnatural attachment to his patient?

Zoë Lindstrom—Is she truly a psychic with the ability to "hear" messages from beyond, or merely a clever shyster?

Chapter One

After weeks of gloomy weather, the sun finally broke over the Olympic Mountains and danced in flames across the steely waters of Puget Sound. There was even a rainbow arching like a mystical doorway over the bay. It was one of those golden, fleeting days that Seattle-ites celebrate and revere, and it was in that moment of sparkling sunlight and glimmering rainbows that Elizabeth Blackstone decided to divorce her husband.

"How do you think he'll take it?" her friend and business partner, Frankie Novak, asked, concerned. To take advantage of the glorious weather, they'd strolled from their shop in Pioneer Square to a trendy new restaurant on the waterfront that Frankie had been dying to try. Instead of being seated at one of the coveted tables with a view, however, they'd been led to what Frankie called the second-tier seating area. The tables along the windows overlooking the bay were reserved for the business moguls and the high-tech movers and shakers that dominated Seattle's economy. An unknown fashion designer and a struggling entrepreneur hardly rated first-tier seating in the city's hottest new restaurant.

"It won't come as that much of a surprise," Elizabeth said in answer to Frankie's question. "We may still live in the same house, but we've been separated for months. Things haven't been the same since…" *Say it,* a little voice commanded. *Say his name.*

Frankie reached over and put her hand over Elizabeth's. "I know. But divorce is never easy, especially after everything else you've been through. Aren't you…" Now it was Frankie who trailed off uncomfortably.

"Aren't I what?"

Frankie shrugged. "You and Paul have been married forever. Aren't you afraid of being alone?"

But I'm already alone, Elizabeth wanted to tell her. Living by herself couldn't possibly be as lonely as living with a man who no longer loved her. Paul still cared for her in his own way, she supposed, but the passion and closeness had long since been spent.

"I'll survive," she said numbly. She always did. Somehow.

Frankie stabbed a prawn in her spinach salad and took a moment to savor the seafood morsel. "Still, you have to wonder what he's going to say, don't you?"

"I don't expect he'll say much of anything." Elizabeth toyed with her pear salad. "He'll probably move out and then he'll have his lawyer contact my lawyer to negotiate an equitable distribution of the assets."

"Are you so sure it will be all that equitable?"

Elizabeth glanced up. "What do you mean?"

"Paul has a lot more to lose in a divorce settlement than you do. He's a rich man, at least on paper. Financial and real-estate holdings, investment deals, retirement and savings accounts, 401(k)s…you think he's going to want to split all that evenly with you?" Frankie leaned forward. "Look, I know he's basically a good guy, but divorce can bring out the worst in people. Especially greed. Believe me, I know. My poor sister got taken to the cleaners when she and her husband split up." Frankie grimaced as she picked up her wineglass. "You need to look out for your own best interests. Take my advice and hire yourself a shark. Because I'll bet you anything *he* will."

"You're assuming that I want half of everything," Elizabeth said with a scowl. "I don't. I'll take the condo, and he can have the lake house. We'll each keep our cars, split the savings and the rest is his."

"And you think he'll go for that?"

"Why wouldn't he? It's more than fair."

"Fair has nothing to do with it. He's a man, so his ego is going to get all tangled up in the negotiations, particularly if he doesn't want this divorce. All I'm saying is that you have to protect yourself." Frankie sipped her wine. "What about the shop?"

"What about it?"

"Need I remind you that it was Paul who bailed us out last year when we were having cash-flow problems after the Nordstrom deal put us in a bind? What if he decides to call in the loan? The last three quarters have looked good, but we're in no shape to cough up that kind of capital right now. We'd have to sell."

"He won't do that," Elizabeth said firmly. "Paul isn't a vengeful person. He's just…"

"A savvy businessman? A husband scorned? Take it from me, that's a dangerous combination," Frankie said. "At least, for us."

"He won't call in the loan. He has no interest in the shop, and besides…" Elizabeth glanced down at her barely touched salad. "I'm thinking of selling my partnership anyway."

Frankie laid down her fork and glared at Elizabeth. "What did you just say?"

Elizabeth sighed. "I didn't mean to spring it on you like that, but…I'm thinking of moving back to Chicago once the divorce is final."

"For God's sakes, *why?*" Frankie demanded. "Why would you do that? You haven't lived there since college, and your family has all moved away since then. They're scattered all over the country. You said so yourself. What's back in Chicago? All your friends are here in Seattle. Not to mention your business."

And so were her memories. Elizabeth rubbed her forehead where a headache started to pound. "It's not definite. Just an idea I've been toying with. I need a change, that's all."

"You're getting a divorce. Isn't that enough of a change?"

Yes, maybe. But maybe what she needed more than a change was a clean break. A new start in a place familiar enough that she wouldn't feel lost, but one in which memories didn't lurk around every corner.

But the past would always be with her, no matter where she went. She would always have memories of her son, and that was the way it should be. Elizabeth wanted to remember Damon…the sound of his voice, his laugh, his hurried footfalls on Christmas morning. She wanted to remember everything about him, but more than anything she wanted to be able to look at his picture and say his name without going to pieces.

She wanted to remember Paul, too, but the way he used to be, when they were happy. Not the cold, steely-eyed stranger who had moved out of her bedroom months ago.

The death of their son had affected them both so deeply they were like different people now. For Elizabeth, the changes were more profound than even Dr. Summers knew, because there were some things she couldn't confide even to her therapist, and certainly not to Paul. Like how she could still sense her son's presence, so strongly at times that she would find herself calling out his name. Like how when she went for walks, she could feel him beside her, could even smell the unique scent of him, all dirt, sunshine and little boy.

Those moments were private and special and Elizabeth savored them. She didn't want to share them with anyone, not even Paul, because he wouldn't understand.

He might think that she was losing her grip on reality and have her committed…again.

So, no, she couldn't tell Paul. She couldn't tell Frankie or Dr. Summers. She couldn't tell anyone.

But there were other times, other moments that Elizabeth didn't savor. Sometimes when she was alone in the apartment, she would hear doors closing and music playing in her dead son's bedroom. Going inside, she would find toys scattered about as if he'd been hurriedly called away in the middle of a game.

It was during those times that Elizabeth would sense another presence.

Someone who seemed to be watching her.

Someone who had been with her ever since she'd awakened from a coma eighteen months ago.

No, Elizabeth most certainly did not savor those moments. She'd come to dread them. And that was why she'd decided to make some changes in her life. Obviously her subconscious was warning her that she couldn't continue in the same vein. She had to come to grips with reality. She had to accept what had happened to her son and to her marriage. She had to try and find a way to be at peace again, because trapped in the depths of despair was no way to live.

"Elizabeth?"

She glanced across the table at Frankie. "I'm sorry. Did you say something?"

"I was just asking if you're okay. You seemed a million miles away just now."

"I'm fine." She blotted her lips on her napkin.

Frankie checked her watch. "We should probably get back. Although Wednesday afternoons are always slow. I don't suppose there's any real need to hurry."

Elizabeth scooted back her chair. "Let me visit the ladies' room and then I'll be ready to go."

"Take your time." Frankie's concerned gaze searched Elizabeth's face. "I'll pay the check when it comes."

THE LOW RUMBLE OF VOICES unnerved Elizabeth as she maneuvered her way through the maze of tables to the front of the restaurant. She had that uncomfortable feeling of being watched, but when she turned once to scan the crowded room, no one even seemed aware of her.

It was just her imagination, she decided. The conversation with Frankie had left her understandably anxious. She dreaded telling Paul what she'd decided, but she knew she couldn't put it off any longer. He would probably be relieved, and Elizabeth had to wonder if that was what she dreaded the most.

The lounge area outside the ladies' room was furnished with an upholstered bench and a pay phone which began to ring as Elizabeth entered through the arched doorway. Pausing, she glanced around to see if anyone hurried to answer it, but when no one came, she ignored it herself and pushed open the door to the ladies' room.

Turning on the water at one of the sinks, she washed her hands, then moistened a paper towel and held it to her face, wincing at the dark circles under her eyes, the fine lines in her face that hadn't been there eighteen months ago.

She didn't look like herself anymore, which was fitting, she supposed. She wasn't herself. She wasn't the same Elizabeth Blackstone who had taken her eyes off the road long enough for a drunk driver to swerve into her lane, hitting her vehicle head-on.

The doctors had later told her that it was not uncommon to suffer short-term amnesia following a trauma. She might never remember the details of the crash, but after a while everything had come back to her…Damon buckled into the front seat beside her, screaming a warning because he saw the car first. And then her own scream. The sound of brakes squealing, metal crunching and her heartbeat pounding in her ears.

Later, the sirens. She'd been told that she hadn't been conscious when the paramedics arrived, but she remembered their voices, their frantic shouts as they used the Jaws of Life to pry her and Damon from the car. She had been floating above it all, conscious on some level but helpless to change the outcome.

When they finally got them free of the twisted metal, she knew when a policeman covered Damon with a sheet. The paramedics were frantically working on her, and she wanted to scream at them to leave her alone and go help her son. But it was too late. Damon was gone. And Elizabeth had wanted to die, too.

She almost had. She'd lingered in a coma for over a

week, and when she'd finally awakened, Paul had been standing by her bed. But he wasn't the same person either. The man at her bedside wasn't the Paul she had kissed goodbye the morning of the accident. That Paul was lost to her forever, and in his place was a remote, grief-stricken stranger. The same stranger she had been living with for the past year and a half.

The door opened and an attractive redhead came in. She wore a pencil skirt and silk blouse accessorized with a simple gold chain and black high heels, the kind of classy yet sexy outfit that Elizabeth might once have worn for her husband.

Her gaze met Elizabeth's in the mirror as she took out her lipstick and began to repair her makeup. "Beautiful day, isn't it?"

"Gorgeous," Elizabeth agreed.

"It's the kind of day that makes you glad to be in love," the woman said with a laugh. "Have a good one," she called as Elizabeth started out the door.

The moment she came out of the bathroom, the pay phone in the lounge area started to ring again. Once again she paused. When no one came this time, she walked over and picked up the receiver. "Hello?"

"Elizabeth."

Her whispered name sent a chill up her spine as the blood in her veins turned to ice.

Without thinking, Elizabeth slammed down the phone and spun, expecting to find someone standing behind her. Reaching out for her.

No one was there. But as she stood motionless, the bathroom door opened and the young woman came out. She had her cell phone in one hand, but instead of making a call, she headed back out to the restaurant.

The pay phone started to ring again.

Elizabeth whirled back around and stared at it for a moment, then snatched it up. "Hello?"

"I think I have a wrong number," a masculine voice said with a sigh. "You're not Carol, are you?"

"No. This is a pay phone at a restaurant."

"Sorry to have bothered you."

"No bother," she mumbled and hung up.

Whatever had possessed her to answer the phone in the first place? Elizabeth wondered as she walked back to her table. And why had she thought she'd heard her name when she first answered?

Obviously she was hearing things. Slamming doors. Music coming from Damon's room. And now her name, whispered in a voice that sent another chill up her spine just thinking about it.

Yes, it was definitely time to make a change in her life.

Even though cell phones were taboo in the dining room, Elizabeth could see that Frankie was talking on hers as she approached the table. She quickly ended the call when she saw Elizabeth. "Hey, I was just talking to…" Her words trailed off. "What's wrong?"

Elizabeth barely heard her. Her attention was focused on one of the tables by the window, where the woman she'd seen in the restroom had just sat down with a dark-haired companion. The woman was laughing and leaning in intimately to hang on his every word. He had his back to Elizabeth, but when he turned to signal the waiter, she recognized his profile. It was Paul.

It's the kind of day that makes you glad to be in love.

As the woman's words came back to her, Elizabeth's heart began to pound in slow, painful beats. She couldn't seem to move. She stood mesmerized by the sight of her husband with another woman.

Frankie followed her gaze and then gasping slightly, stood and grabbed Elizabeth's arm. "Come on, honey. Let's get out of here."

She kept a firm hold on Elizabeth's arm as she led her out of the restaurant and then, once they were on the street, she started to swear.

Elizabeth said nothing.

Her tirade finally over, Frankie swiped back her black hair. "Okay, I feel better." She gave Elizabeth a sympathetic look. "You know I'd like to go in there and give that bastard a piece of my mind, don't you? But we have to keep things in perspective. It's not the end of the world. You're going to divorce him anyway. Granted, he should have let the ink dry on the final decree before he got himself a hot, young girlfriend...." She swore again and clapped a hand to her mouth. "I can't believe I just said that. I'm sorry, Lizzy."

Elizabeth shrugged. "It's okay."

"No, it's not okay. The man's a pig, but show me one who isn't. Let's just try to look on the bright side here.

If he's got a girlfriend, he's not going to want to make waves about the settlement. That gives you leverage. Power." Frankie's brown eyes gleamed in the sunlight. "You can stick it to him but good after this."

She was right, Elizabeth tried to tell herself. She and Paul were getting a divorce, so what did it matter if he was already seeing someone else? He was a young, handsome, successful businessman. Elizabeth hadn't expected him to be on the market forever. It would have been nice if he'd waited, as Frankie said, until the ink was dry on the divorce papers, but in the long run it didn't change anything.

So why did she feel so hurt? So utterly devastated and betrayed? Paul had a right to find happiness. They both did.

It's okay, she kept telling herself over and over. It was going to be okay.

"Let's just get back to the shop," Frankie said. "We can talk about it there."

Elizabeth hesitated. She didn't want to talk about what she'd just seen. Not yet. It was too fresh. Too confusing. "I think I'll just walk around for a while. You don't mind, do you? As you said, Wednesdays are usually pretty slow."

"Of course I don't mind," Frankie said. "Wednesdays are dull as dirt, so Karen and I can definitely hold down the fort. It's just…I hate to leave you alone."

"I'm fine," Elizabeth assured her. She even managed to muster up a smile. "I just need some fresh air. I'll be back in a little while."

Frankie nodded. "I'll see you back at the shop.

Lizzy…" She reached out and put her hand on Elizabeth's arm. "It really is going to be okay, you know."

"I know."

But it wasn't okay. No matter how many times Elizabeth tried to tell herself otherwise, her life was never going to be okay again. Her son was dead and her husband was seeing another woman.

As she stared at the restaurant, a breeze from the water drifted through her hair, lifting it as though an invisible hand caressed it.

Shivering uncontrollably, Elizabeth turned and walked away.

Chapter Two

She'd been waiting in the coffee shop across from Paul's building for nearly half an hour when she finally spotted his silver Lexus pull into the attached parking garage.

Giving him a few more minutes, Elizabeth finished her coffee, then tossed the disposable cup in the trash can as she left the shop and crossed the street to the office building. When she got off the elevator on the thirty-second floor, the receptionist greeted her warmly.

"Elizabeth! I was just thinking the other day how long it's been since I've seen you. How are you?"

"I'm fine, Angie, thanks. And you?"

"Can't complain," the older woman said with a smile.

"How's your mother?" Elizabeth asked. "The last time we spoke, she was going in for surgery. A problem with her back, wasn't it?"

"Oh, goodness me, that was ages ago. How nice of you to remember. Mother's doing well for someone her age. She's eighty-six, you know. She'll probably outlive me, the rate she's going. I'll be sure and tell her you asked about her."

"Yes, please give her my best." Elizabeth paused. "Is my— Is Paul in?"

"I just saw him come back from lunch a few minutes ago. Do you want me to ring him?"

"I'd rather just go on back, if that's okay."

"Oh, sure." Angie waved toward the corridor to the right of her desk. "You know the way."

Elizabeth rounded the corner to Paul's office, then stopped dead. The redhead from the restaurant sat behind the desk outside Paul's door. She was on the phone, and when Elizabeth first saw her, she wanted to turn and walk quickly away. But the woman glanced up just then and her smile disappeared. She recognized Elizabeth. It was there in her eyes, but for some reason she pretended not to.

"Yes? May I help you?" she asked briskly.

"I'd like to see Mr. Blackstone."

She reached for the phone. "Your name?"

"Elizabeth Blackstone."

"Oh, Mrs. Blackstone…I didn't know it was you." The woman stared at Elizabeth in a way that was completely unnerving. A mixture of curiosity, disdain and…pity. Or perhaps that was only her imagination, Elizabeth decided.

"No reason you should. I don't believe we've ever met."

The woman stood and offered Elizabeth her hand. "I'm Nina Wilson. Paul's—Mr. Blackstone's assistant."

Elizabeth reluctantly took her hand, wondering what had happened to Paul's last assistant, Ariel. She'd been young and attractive, too, but happily married, with two kids. This woman's left hand was bare, and judging by her trim, shapely figure, Elizabeth seriously doubted that she'd had children. At least, not recently.

"Is my husband in?" Why hadn't she just called him Paul? Elizabeth wondered. Was she still trying to stake her claim? If so, how pathetic was that?

"I'll buzz him and tell him you're here." Another emotion glimmered in the woman's eyes, one Elizabeth couldn't define this time.

"No, don't bother," Elizabeth said with a cool smile. "I'll just pop in for a moment."

She could feel the woman's gaze on her as she walked away and she knew that if she turned, Nina Wilson would be staring at her.

Elizabeth knocked, then waited for Paul to say, "Come in," before she opened the door and stepped inside. He was standing at the wall of windows, looking out at the mountains. Hands shoved in his pockets, he appeared to be a million miles away.

"Did Carter ever call back?" he asked absently.

Elizabeth cleared her throat. "I guess you were expecting someone else."

At the sound of her voice he spun, a look of astonishment flashing across his handsome features.

It wasn't fair, Elizabeth thought fleetingly. It wasn't

fair that after everything they'd been through, after all the grief and hurt and bitterness of the past eighteen months, he still had the power to take her breath away.

"Elizabeth! What are you…what brings you by here?"

He chose his words carefully around her, Elizabeth noticed. They'd both been walking on eggshells for so long, she wondered if either of them even knew how to relax anymore.

Coming over to stand behind his desk, his gray eyes raked her curiously. And no wonder. She hadn't been in his office in over a year. Not since before the accident.

"I was out walking, taking advantage of the beautiful weather, and I found myself near your building," she tried to say in a normal voice. But what was normal these days? "I decided to drop by and see if you have dinner plans." *Oh, God.* She hadn't meant it to sound that way, as if she were asking him out.

He lifted a brow as he regarded her across the expanse of the desk. For the longest moment he said nothing, and Elizabeth rushed to explain, "There's… something I need to talk to you about."

"I see." His gaze flickered, but she didn't have a clue what he was thinking. He seemed so remote, so cold. Nothing at all like the man who had barely let her out of bed on their honeymoon.

She didn't want to remember their honeymoon now, though. Or the night they'd made Damon. Not with Nina Wilson sitting right outside Paul's door.

"Shall I pick up something on my way home?" he finally asked.

"No, I'll cook." It would give her something to do for the rest of the afternoon.

"Are you sure?"

She hadn't cooked in months, but Elizabeth found herself looking forward to the prospect. "I'll enjoy puttering around the kitchen again."

"In that case, what time?"

"Seven-thirty? Is that too early?" He often didn't get home until well after ten. And even on those nights he didn't go straight to bed but would sit in the living room with a drink, sometimes watching television, sometimes staring into the dark.

He nodded. "I'll make sure to get away early. I'll see you at seven-thirty."

He came around the desk then to walk her to the door. His shoulder brushed against hers, and Elizabeth was surprised to find herself growing quite breathless again. She could smell his cologne, a rich, classy scent with seductive undertones. Yes, that was Paul. Rich, classy, seductive...

The dark gray pin-striped suit he had on was one of her favorites. But then, Paul could wear anything and look good. He was tall and slender, his body toned from the miles and miles of running he did every week. At thirty-six, he had the physique of a man a decade younger, but the lines around his mouth and eyes gave his face maturity.

Elizabeth had never met any man—and never would, she suspected—who compared in any way to Paul Blackstone.

At the door he gazed down at her, and it was almost as if…for a moment it seemed as if he might…

The door opened and Nina Wilson came in. "Boyd Carter is on line two—" She stopped short when she saw Elizabeth, and her expression became contrite. "Oh, I'm sorry. I didn't know you still had someone with you."

"My wife was just leaving."

My wife.

Elizabeth glanced at Nina, and for a moment, the woman's gaze darkened with something that might have been fury. Then she seemed to shrug it off and smiled. "It was nice meeting you…Elizabeth."

Score one for you, Elizabeth thought as she left the office. Because by using her first name, Nina Wilson had effectively put them on equal footing.

As Paul Blackstone watched his wife leave the office, an uneasy premonition tickled along his backbone. So she wanted to have dinner with him tonight. What was that all about?

He wanted to believe that the overture was a good sign. Elizabeth might finally be emerging from the dark place she'd crawled into eighteen months ago. Somehow he didn't think so, though.

He understood her despair. There had been times in the past year and a half when he'd wanted nothing more than to pull the covers over his head and hide from the world rather than wake up to face another day without his son. But life had to go on. He had a living to make. Mortgage payments, bills, responsibilities that didn't stop because life no longer seemed worth living.

Eventually he'd been able to see the sunlight again. Dimmer, yes, but it was there if he looked hard enough. But Elizabeth...

Paul closed his eyes briefly. He very much feared that she would never find her way out of the darkness, and there wasn't a damn thing he could do about it.

Trying to shake off a growing sense of doom, he took the call from Boyd Carter, but his mind wasn't really on the conversation. When he finally hung up, he swiveled his chair around to stare out the windows. The sun was still shining, but the rainbow over Elliott Bay had long since faded. And in the distance he thought he saw rain clouds gathering over the snowy peak of Mount Olympus.

He let his mind retreat back to the visit from his wife. What did she want to talk to him about? Reconciliation? A fresh start?

Wishful thinking, he decided. He was fairly certain that she'd decided it was time to end the travesty that their marriage had become. And maybe she was right. Maybe it was time to let go. Maybe it had been time over a year ago when she'd sobbed in his arms that she didn't want to go on. That without their son she had nothing to live for.

Paul understood her grief. He did. But, God, how that had hurt him. How it still hurt him that she hadn't been able to turn to him for comfort, but instead had pushed him away.

But as devastated and grief-stricken as he'd been that night, the worst had been yet to come. A few days later he'd gotten home from work to find Elizabeth unconscious in their bed. Unable to rouse her, he'd called the paramedics, and they'd rushed her to the hospital, where the sleeping pills had been pumped from her stomach.

When she'd finally awakened a few hours later and seen Paul at her bedside, she'd slipped her hand from his and turned away.

She'd blamed him for saving her. Blamed him for pulling her back from the darkness.

"Why can't you just let me go?" she'd whispered in despair.

Because I love you, he'd wanted to tell her. *Because you mean everything to me.*

Instead he'd turned and walked out of the room, and nothing had been the same between them since.

Elizabeth had been moved into the psychiatric ward later that same day and had begun sessions with Dr. Julian Summers, a specialist in grief therapy who had come very highly recommended.

She'd responded to treatment almost at once. It was like a miracle. Almost overnight the color had returned to her cheeks, her eyes had lost that vacant look and she'd even put on a few of the pounds she'd lost after the accident. Paul had begun to hope for the best, but when she'd come home a few weeks later, she was a changed woman. The breakdown had made her stronger in a lot of ways, but she was no longer the woman Paul had married. She'd become a polite stranger who shared his apartment and even his bed, but one who had no desire to share her life with him.

Paul hadn't known what to do or say to get her back. The worst thing he could do was pressure her in any way, Dr. Summers had warned him. So he'd backed off. He'd given her the space she seemed to want and need. What else could he do? And the next thing he knew, the chasm between them had grown so wide he didn't have a clue how to breach it.

Maybe he hadn't tried hard enough to reach her, Paul thought now as he rubbed the back of his neck. In some respects, it had been easier to let her drift away than to fight his way back to her. He'd had his own grief to cope with. His own guilt.

And now Elizabeth was ready to end it.

He knew it. He could *feel* it. They'd become strangers, but in some ways—important ways—he still knew her so well. They'd been together for thirteen years, and during that time he'd learned to read her expressions and interpret her body language. The nervous flutter of her hands always meant something was on her mind. Something important.

She was going to ask him for a divorce tonight, and there wasn't a damn thing he could do about that either.

Maybe it was what he wanted, too, Paul decided. He was tired of walking on eggshells. Tired of the loneliness. The silence. The grief that never seemed to lose its grip on his heart.

It would be nice to have someone to go out to dinner with again. Someone with whom he could share a leisurely Saturday afternoon.

It would be nice to have a woman in his arms again. He and Elizabeth hadn't been together in over a year, and he wasn't cut out for the life of a celibate.

He sometimes still found it hard to believe how far apart they'd drifted when they'd once been so close. They'd had what he'd always considered the perfect marriage. Friends first, then lovers. They'd done everything together, shared so much of themselves with one another that it had been hard to tell where he ended and she began.

The birth of their son had changed all that, in a good way for the most part. But there had been times after Damon was born that Paul had missed the closeness he and Elizabeth had once shared. He'd missed the times when they'd been able to throw a few things in a suitcase and go off for a spur-of-the-moment weekend without having to worry about soccer games and birthday parties. He'd missed the quiet evenings alone. The Sunday mornings in bed.

Those times of discontent had been rare because Paul had loved his son more than anything. And when Damon died, a part of him had died, too. He'd been consumed, not just by grief but with a killing guilt for having longed, however briefly, for a time without his son.

And now he was losing Elizabeth, too. In truth, he'd already lost her. She'd slipped away from him the moment she'd opened her eyes in the hospital, but now he supposed it was time to make it official.

Unless…

He spun back to his desk and picked up the invitation he'd received in the mail that morning.

You are cordially invited for a weekend of rejuvenation at the Fernhaven Hotel…a heavenly retreat deep in the heart of the Cascade Mountains…

Rejuvenation.

Perhaps that was what they both needed right now.

Chapter Three

Elizabeth left the shop in Pioneer Square early that afternoon and headed west on First Avenue, stopping briefly at Pike Place Market for fresh salmon and produce. Normally she liked to linger at the market and watch the tourists' reactions to the fish throwers or dash in for a quick cup of coffee at the original Starbucks, but today she made her purchases quickly and headed back up First Avenue to their condo in Belltown.

Letting herself inside, she tossed the mail onto the console table in the hallway, then put away the groceries.

Late-afternoon sunlight flooded through the windows in the living room and drew her outside to the balcony, where she stood watching the ferries return from Bainbridge Island. The condo was a rare northwest-corner unit, so they didn't get the morning light, but the view of Elliott Bay and the Olympic Mountains was more than worth it.

In an hour or so the sun would set and the lights along the waterfront would twinkle on. Elizabeth loved

Seattle by night. They had a partial view of the downtown skyline from their dining room window, and she used to sit there and watch the skyscrapers come to life while she waited for Paul and Damon to get home. And then the door would finally burst open and Damon would come charging in, excited about soccer practice or a Mariners game he and Paul had tickets for. Paul would come in behind him, smiling indulgently, the proud father…the loving husband as he came over to brush his lips against Elizabeth's.

Then they would all sit at the table together and have dinner, usually something kid-friendly—spaghetti, hamburgers, pizza. But sometimes they'd have a grown-up meal of seafood and salad, and she and Paul would share a bottle of wine over candlelight.

After dinner they'd watch TV for a while and then later, with Damon tucked in bed, she and Paul would finish off the wine on the balcony as they watched the boats in the harbor. Occasionally they'd see a cruise ship putting out to sea, and the sound of the foghorn—the final goodbye—always made Elizabeth feel lost and forlorn. But with Paul's arm around her, the loneliness passed quickly.

Sometimes in bed at night, nestled in his arms, she would stay awake thinking about how lucky she was. She had everything any woman could possibly want—a wonderful husband, a beautiful son, a gorgeous home. She even had a promising career as a local fashion designer. And then it had all gone away. Just like that. In the space of a heartbeat, she had taken her eyes off the road to smile at something Damon said…and she'd lost everything.

The home was still there. Paul was still there…for now. Her career was even flourishing. But nothing was ever going to be the same again.

Elizabeth rubbed her hands up and down her arms. Now that the sun was setting, she could feel a chill in the breeze that blew in from the bay and she turned to go back inside. A draft slammed the door shut behind her before she could pull it closed, and the crash caused her to jump.

The wind swept some of the mail off the table in the hallway, and she hurried over to pick it up. Glancing through the stack, she paused on a thick, creamy envelope addressed to Mr. and Mrs. Paul Blackstone. The return address was Fernhaven Hotel.

Elizabeth knew about the place. It was a recently built luxury hotel in the Cascade Mountains. Paul's brokerage firm had been instrumental in putting the deal together for the owners. On his recommendation, Frankie Loves Johnny—Elizabeth and Frankie's boutique—had landed the contract to design most of the staff uniforms. It wasn't couture, but the deal had been financially lucrative and had helped the shop regain its financial footing after an arrangement with a major retailer had drained much of their operating capital. That, and the loan from Paul, of course.

Elizabeth slit open the envelope and extracted the brochure and invitation inside.

You are cordially invited for a weekend of rejuvenation at the Fernhaven Hotel...a heavenly retreat deep in the heart of the Cascade Mountains...

The invitation went on to explain that, in appreciation of their contribution to Fernhaven, she and Paul would be pampered guests at a preopening celebration. The official opening was still some weeks away, so the complimentary weekend would be a dry run for the staff.

Elizabeth set aside the invitation and picked up the brochure. She'd seen pictures of the old hotel—it had burned down over seventy years ago—along with photos of the staff and some of the guests. Her designs had been inspired by the original uniforms, much as the architecture of the new hotel, with its gray facade and spired roofline, had been modeled after the first one.

Nestled deep within one of the Pacific Northwest's magnificent rain forests, Fernhaven wore a mantle of mystery, due in part to its tragic history, but also because of its isolation. Even the deeply shaded grounds looked foreboding, and yet there was also something appealing about the place. Something that seemed to beckon even from the photograph...

The back of her neck tingled in that all-too-familiar manner, and Elizabeth spun toward the balcony doors, the brochure drifting from her fingers. She caught her breath. For one split second she could have sworn someone was on the balcony staring in at her.

Her hand flew to her heart. The figure on the balcony

did the same, and then Elizabeth realized that she was seeing her own reflection in the glass.

Laughing nervously, she put away the mail and went into the kitchen to grill the salmon and prepare a salad.

By seven-thirty they had sat down to eat. Paul had gotten home early and changed from his suit into jeans and a black V-neck sweater that she'd given him for his birthday a couple of years ago. Elizabeth wondered if he'd selected it for any particular reason, but then decided that her own anxiety was making her read too much into his actions. He'd always said the sweater was one of his favorites.

They made small, meaningless talk during the meal, and when they were finished, Paul got up and went into the kitchen to grab the bottle of wine. Replenishing both their glasses, he sat back down.

"That was an excellent meal, Elizabeth. You haven't lost your touch."

"Thanks. It's like riding a bike, I guess." She picked up her wineglass, took a sip and choked a little.

"Are you all right?"

"I'm…fine…" She trailed off nervously and returned her glass to the table.

"So what did you want to talk to me about?" Paul's eyes gleamed darkly in the candlelight, and for a moment Elizabeth couldn't tear her gaze away. "Elizabeth?"

She moistened her lips. "I want to talk about…us. Our…arrangement." She hesitated. "It's not working, Paul. For either of us."

"Arrangement?" He frowned. "Do you mean our marriage?"

"Yes." She drew a breath. "I want a divorce."

"A divorce," he repeated in a voice she'd never heard him use before. She couldn't quite figure out what it meant.

She sucked in another breath. "Our marriage isn't working, and it hasn't been for a long time. What we once had...is gone. We can't get it back. It's no one's fault. We just have to accept it."

"As easy as that."

"Nothing about this is easy," she said on a whisper. "But I can't go on this way. It's too painful. I'd rather...it would better for both of us if we just...made a clean break."

"So you not only want a divorce, you also want a clean break. How do you plan to accomplish that?" His gaze deepened as he stared at her over the candlelight.

"I'm thinking of moving back to Chicago," she said.

One brow lifted slightly. "Really? And what does your business partner have to say about your plans? Or haven't you told her yet?"

"We've discussed it briefly." Elizabeth paused. "Nothing's definite. I haven't made any firm decisions. All I know is that—"

"You want a divorce."

"Yes." When he said nothing else, Elizabeth glanced at him. "Surely you don't want to go on like this either. If you were free, you could start a new life. You could find someone else. Maybe…you already have," she said hesitantly.

If possible, his expression grew even darker. "Just what are you implying, Elizabeth?"

She couldn't do it after all, Elizabeth discovered. She couldn't confront him with what she'd seen earlier that day. Because she didn't want to see the truth in his eyes, she supposed.

But she couldn't hide from the image. It came back to her now, and she had to swallow back a wave of panic. Paul and another woman…

She closed her eyes for a moment, willing away the image. "I'm not implying anything. I just thought that if you were free, you might meet someone else. Someone who could be the kind of wife to you that you need."

"Please don't presume to know what I need." He scooted back his chair and stood abruptly. It was the first time he'd shown any emotion during the conversation, and his anger seemed to take him by surprise. He strode into the kitchen for a moment, and when he came back out, he had his feelings firmly under control. His expression was a mask of indifference as he stood behind his chair, gazing down at her. "Just answer one question for me."

"Of course. If I can."

"Do you still love me?"

The question caught Elizabeth off guard and hit her like a fist to her solar plexus. Breathless, she glanced down at her laced fingers. She couldn't look at Paul when she answered. "I'll always love you. But it isn't enough anymore."

"That's such a cliché," he said bitterly.

And now it was Elizabeth who felt a quick stab of anger. "It's a cliché because it happens to be the truth! I do love you, Paul, but I'm not…I can't be married to you anymore. It hurts too much. Every time I look at you…" She trailed off and put a trembling hand to her mouth.

"You see our son."

She nodded. "And every time you look at me, you must think of the accident. You have to ask yourself over and over why I chose that moment to take my eyes off the road."

"You're wrong." He clenched his fists at his sides. "I've never blamed you for what happened. No one was at fault except the drunken bastard who decided to get behind the wheel of his car that day."

"But if I hadn't looked away—"

"Elizabeth, don't. We can't change the past."

"I know that. But we can change the future. We can try to salvage something of our lives. You deserve to be happy, Paul. We both do."

"And you think a divorce will make us happy?"

Elizabeth shook her head helplessly. "I don't know. All I do know is that I can't go on like this."

He turned away for a moment, running his hand through his dark hair. When he looked back at her, his eyes had gone so cold and distant that Elizabeth wanted to cry. "All right. You can have your divorce. I won't try to stop you. You can have the condo, the savings, whatever you want." When she started to protest, his dark gaze silenced her. "But I am going to need something from you."

An edge in his voice made her frown. "What is it?"

He shrugged. "A little time, that's all. I'm in the middle of negotiations for another multimillion-dollar hotel, and for a number of reasons some of the investors are getting skittish. If even one of them pulls out, it could have a domino effect on the others. And if they get wind that my personal life is in upheaval, they might lose faith in my ability to put this deal together. I don't want that to happen. I *can't* let it happen. My career is on the line here, Elizabeth, so I'm going to need you to put the divorce proceedings on hold for the time being."

Elizabeth's frown deepened. "For how long?"

"A couple of weeks. A month at the most. It's not much to ask, is it?"

"No, I suppose not." Although now that the decision was made, Elizabeth just wanted it over and done with. "Will you be staying here until then?"

He shrugged again. "My moving out would defeat the purpose, wouldn't it?" He smiled over the flickering candles, but there was no humor in his dark eyes. "The investor I'm most concerned about is a man named Boyd Carter. He was one of the major backers in the Fernhaven project and he'll be at the retreat next weekend, along with some of the potential investors."

"The preopening celebration, you mean. I saw the invitation earlier," Elizabeth said.

"One came here?" He seemed surprised by that. "I received one at the office, too. I suspect you and Frankie will be getting one at the shop. At any rate, if I can get a few moments alone with Carter, I think I can allay his concerns. Once he's sold on the deal, the others will fall in line. If everything goes the way I expect it to, you can file for divorce as soon as we get back."

She stared at him for a moment. "When *we* get back?"

"I'm hoping that you'll go with me. Carter is big on family. If we're seen together—"

"Wait a minute," Elizabeth said in dismay. "You want me to convince him that we have a happy marriage just so you can work a deal with him? That's ridiculous. And dishonest."

"I'm not asking you to lie," Paul said coolly. "And, yes, it is ridiculous that in this day and age my personal life should come under scrutiny before a relic like Carter will do business with me. But that's just the way it is." His gaze met hers. "All I'm asking is for you to spend the weekend at Fernhaven with me. You don't have to put on an act. Just be yourself. Do you think you could do that much for me?"

"I don't—"

She'd been about to refuse. Going away for a weekend together was no way to start a separation. But before she could get the words out, the balcony door flew open, startling them both as the draft blew out the candles.

Elizabeth gave a tiny surprised cry, but Paul merely flipped on a light and went over to investigate the door.

"The latch is sticking," he muttered as he closed the door. "I'll need to get someone here to fix it before we leave." He tried the door a few more times, then glanced up. "What do you say, Elizabeth? Do we have a deal?"

"Yes," she said on a sigh. "We have a deal."

But that wasn't what she'd meant to say at all.

Chapter Four

One week later...

The drive from Seattle to Fernhaven took longer than Elizabeth expected, but the scenery along the way was magnificent. The weather had been warm and sunny when they'd left the city, but as they reached Mount Baker, the sun disappeared and a fine mist descended over the car. She could feel the outside temperature dropping and she reached in the backseat for her jacket.

"I can turn on the heater if you're cold," Paul offered.

"No, that's okay. I just need something on my arms."

"You're sure?"

"Yes, I'm fine." She seemed to be saying that a lot lately, and Elizabeth wondered if anyone who knew her would ever be truly convinced that she was well now. Or at least on the road to recovery.

Ever since her breakdown she'd been treated with kid gloves by everyone around her. Her family, her friends, her business partner. But especially her husband. Sometimes the way Paul looked at her set Elizabeth's teeth on edge. It was almost as if he was waiting for the other shoe to drop.

She understood their concern. In her darkest hour she'd taken an overdose of sleeping pills, but that had been over a year ago. And Elizabeth couldn't honestly say that she'd meant to end her own life. She'd been in a bad place, that was for sure, but she was much stronger now. Even though there were still times when she worried about her mental stability, she suspected that the music, the slamming doors and the scattered toys in Damon's room were all signs from her subconscious that she hadn't fully accepted her son's death yet.

Elizabeth also knew that she would never again try to take her own life. She wouldn't do that to the people who loved her. Life was precious, even without Damon. It just wasn't the same.

Rousing herself from her reverie, she realized that she and Paul had spoken very little during the trip. The two-hour car ride was a mirror of the way the past week had gone. They'd avoided each other as much as possible. Elizabeth made sure she stayed in the bedroom until she heard Paul leave for work in the mornings and then she usually turned in before he got home. Which wasn't hard to do since he'd been putting in a lot of long days. She wanted to believe that he was at the office getting ready for this trip, but she still couldn't get the image of Paul and Nina Wilson out of her head.

She told herself repeatedly that Paul's relationship

with the woman was none of her business. She'd asked him for a divorce. He could do what he wanted.

But the divorce wasn't final. Far from it. They weren't even separated yet, so technically their marriage license was still binding. To her, at least. No matter how many times she tried to justify Paul's behavior, Elizabeth was still bothered by his seemingly callous disregard of the promises he'd made to her thirteen years ago.

Of course, it was entirely possibly that his relationship with Nina Wilson was a purely professional one. All Elizabeth had to do was ask him. She felt sure that no matter what he said, she'd be able to read the truth in his eyes. But she didn't ask him for one simple reason—she didn't want to know.

Forcing her thoughts away from Paul and Nina Wilson, Elizabeth returned to her reading. She'd brought along the Fernhaven brochure and some of the materials she'd printed from the Internet to study before she'd begun designing the uniforms.

The place had a fascinating, albeit tragic, history. The original hotel had been built in the thirties as a luxury retreat for the rich and famous. On the night of the grand-opening ball a fire broke out and spread through the floors, completely engulfing the main ballroom. Hundreds had perished. At the time it had been a calamity on par with the Titanic and later the Hindenburg, but with the war in Europe heating up and the attack on Pearl Harbor a few years later, the fire and its tragic consequences had been forgotten.

Over the years various parties had expressed interest in rebuilding the hotel, but it wasn't until two years ago that Annika Wallenburg, a descendant of the original owner, had finally gotten the ball rolling.

Paul's firm had been instrumental in bringing the investors together, but it had been a risky venture, to say the least. "Why were you so interested in the Fernhaven project?" Elizabeth asked suddenly.

He lifted a hand from the steering wheel to rub the back of his neck. "Why do you ask?"

"No reason, really. I've been reading about the fire," she explained. "I already knew about it, but I'd forgotten some of the details. Weren't the investors afraid the history of the place might be a little off-putting to prospective guests?"

He glanced at her with a slight smile. "You mean the ghosts?"

"Ghosts?" The back of her neck tingled as she turned to stare at him. "What are you talking about?"

"Fernhaven is supposed to be haunted. Surely you must have run across that little tidbit in all your reading."

"No, I don't think I did," Elizabeth murmured. She gazed out the window for a moment.

No reason Paul's revelation should upset her, she told herself firmly. It was just a legend. Fernhaven wasn't really haunted because ghosts didn't exit. There was a perfectly logical explanation for everything that had happened to her in the past eighteen months. Grief could do strange things to a person's mind…

"To answer your question," Paul said, "the fire was seventy years ago, so no, the history of Fernhaven wasn't a particular concern to the investors. But even if it had been, Annika Wallenburg was determined to rebuild the hotel. She would have continued the project with or without outside backing, even if it meant she had to use every cent of her personal fortune."

"Why did it mean so much to her?" Elizabeth asked curiously. "She's a young woman, isn't she? She wasn't even around when the original Fernhaven was built."

"No, but her grandmother, Ingrid, was. Ingrid's engagement to her childhood sweetheart was to be announced on the night of the grand-opening ball. He'd just arrived from Stockholm, where he'd been attending university. They hadn't seen each other in nearly a year. And then the fire broke out. Somehow Ingrid managed to escape, but her fiancé was killed."

"How sad." Elizabeth felt a strange, tragic kinship with the woman, even though she'd never even met her.

"Ingrid later married and had children, but according to Annika, her grandmother never got over her first love. Annika's parents were killed when she was just a child, and her grandmother took her in and raised her. Annika is very devoted to her grandmother and determined to carry out her last wish."

"Which is?"

"That she be allowed to live out the rest of her days at Fernhaven."

"Wow," Elizabeth said. "Building a hotel is quite a tribute, especially considering the financial risks involved."

"Money really wasn't a concern. Annika is a very wealthy woman. Not only is she heiress to the Wallenburg fortune, but she'll also inherit a great deal of money from her grandmother's family. As I said, she would have used her own fortune to rebuild Fernhaven if necessary. However, the business prospectus she put together was a sound one. The location in the Cascades is excellent for skiing in the winter and hiking in the summer, and with the popularity of luxury spas and retreats, Fernhaven's natural hot springs and mineral baths are an extremely marketable attraction. And the scenery is breathtaking. I don't believe there's anything quite like it anywhere in the world."

"You're proud of it," Elizabeth said softly.

He gave her a surprised look. "I guess I am. But now it's on to the next project."

"And Boyd Carter."

His smiled disappeared. "Yes. Boyd Carter could still be a problem, but that's not for you to worry about. Just relax and enjoy the weekend."

Elizabeth started to remind him that she had accompanied him on this trip as a favor, not for pleasure. But what was the point in arguing over such a minor point? Besides, he was right. The scenery was gorgeous, and surprisingly she really was enjoying herself.

As they turned off the main road onto the curving drive, Elizabeth found herself holding her breath in anticipation. And then, as they rounded a turn, Fernhaven materialized like magic before them. Rising out of the mist, the hotel appeared to float like the spirits who supposedly dwelled within the resurrected walls.

The sloping lawn—what she could see of it through the haze—was emerald-green and adorned with topiaries, statues and fountains surrounded by lush dripping ferns. The building itself was multistoried and of a light gray color that blended with the mist. The spired roof and arched windows created a dreamy, fairy-tale feel, but the ornate carvings beneath the ledge were almost gothic. It was a beautiful hotel, mystical and serene, but the shadowy forest lurking in the background gave it an air of foreboding.

Paul slowed the car and Elizabeth stared through the windshield at the hotel.

"Quite a place, isn't it?" he said proudly.

"It's beautiful," Elizabeth breathed. "Magnificent. But…"

"But what?" Paul asked with an edge in his voice.

Elizabeth caressed her arms with her hands. "I don't know. I feel a strange sense of déjà vu. Like I've been here before, but I know I haven't. I guess it must be the pictures I've been studying."

"Actually," Paul said, "you have been here before. You don't remember?"

She turned sharply. "When?" Ever since the accident she'd experienced gaps in her memory. Doctors had told her the condition wasn't unusual after a severe head trauma, but the lapses always took her by surprise.

"We were here a few weeks before the accident," Paul said quietly. "Damon was on a camping trip with Nicholas Braiden and his dad. You and I drove up for the ground-breaking ceremony. You and Frankie had already been given the contract to design the uniforms and you wanted to get a feel for the place."

"It's so strange that I can't remember—" And then it came back to her. They'd driven up on a Friday night and stayed in a nearby bed-and-breakfast. Elizabeth had been both nervous and excited at the prospect of spending a weekend alone with her husband. They'd had dinner at a quiet out-of-the-way restaurant and then gone straight back to the room. After they'd made love, they'd even talked about having another baby.

That night seemed like a dream to Elizabeth. A lovely, distant dream. What seemed more real to her was the ground-breaking ceremony the next day. The ruins had been cleared away by then and bulldozers had leveled the property. She remembered now seeing a man at the service, a tall, aristocratic stranger dressed all in black who'd stood apart from the crowd. He didn't seem to be connected to the ceremony, but Elizabeth had the strongest feeling that he *belonged* there. That he had a purpose for being there. And when his gaze met hers, an odd mixture of fear and excitement had gripped her.

She'd forgotten all about that day. And about the man.

"Elizabeth?"

"I'm fine," she said a bit tersely before Paul could ask if she was all right.

His mouth thinned and he turned his attention back to the road. Pulling to the front of the hotel, he parked the car as two valets came hurrying to open their doors and a bellman took charge of the luggage.

As they walked up the steps, Paul put his hand on Elizabeth's elbow. The gesture was as natural as breathing to him. The slight contact didn't mean anything, but for some reason Elizabeth had the urge to pull away from him…as if someone was *willing* her to pull away.

At the top of the steps she paused to glance over her shoulder. In spite of the mist, a handful of people strolled about the grounds, but no one seemed to notice her. Turning, she followed Paul into the lobby, an opulent, lofty space with marble floors, trickling fountains and sparkling chandeliers.

A clerk wearing a black blazer emblazoned with a tiny green fern leaf smiled as they approached the front desk. "Welcome to Fernhaven. May I have your names, please?"

"Mr. and Mrs. Paul Blackstone."

The clerk typed their names into the computer. After a few moments he asked them to sign the registration form, then produced two keys. "You'll be in guest cottage five," he said. "It's the farthest one from the hotel. Very cozy and private. It even has two fireplaces."

"Guest cottage?" Elizabeth said in surprise. "We aren't staying in the main hotel?"

The clerk seemed to be affronted by her question. "The cottages are extremely desirable, I assure you. We were swamped with requests—"

"Do you have something in the main hotel?" Paul cut in, but Elizabeth quickly put her hand on his arm.

"No, it's okay. I was just surprised, that's all. I didn't realize the hotel had guest cottages," she said to the clerk. "I'm sure they're lovely."

"Number five is an exact replica of the original," he said proudly. "Right down to the linens."

"In that case, I can't wait to see it." Elizabeth tried to muster up the correct amount of enthusiasm to soothe the clerk's ruffled feathers. He appeared somewhat appeased as he finished checking them in.

Another bellman led them across the lobby and through an outside door where golf carts were lined up beneath an awning. Stowing their luggage on the back, he got behind the wheel and waited for Elizabeth and Paul to climb aboard. Then, letting out the clutch, he deftly maneuvered the cart along a narrow, twisting trail past a row of cottages. Elizabeth had to look closely to see them. They were spaced far apart for privacy and set so far back from the trail as to almost disappear in the woodsy setting.

Pulling up in front of the last one, the bellman got out to open the front door. After Elizabeth and Paul entered, he went back out to collect their luggage, which he placed in the master bedroom. Wishing them a pleasant stay, he accepted Paul's discreet tip, then disappeared.

Alone with her husband again, Elizabeth glanced around. The clerk had been right. The cottage was very elegant and charming, furnished in autumn shades of gold, green and terra-cotta. The silk drapery and striped upholstery were luxurious almost to the point of decadence, and when she went to check out the bedroom, she discovered that no detail had been spared in that room either, including logs stacked in the fireplace.

The bed was a large four-poster queen with a soft chenille spread and lots of cloudlike pillows that were instantly inviting. The rest of the furniture was dark and heavy, but the French doors leading out to a private terrace kept the room from being too dark and oppressive.

Elizabeth walked over and opened one of the doors. "I can hear a waterfall," she said absently.

"It's only about a quarter of a mile or so from here," Paul said as he came up behind her. "Just along that trail." He nodded in the direction of the path they'd come up. "Maybe we can hike up and see it tomorrow, if you feel like it."

Elizabeth swallowed back the panic that rose in her throat. Did he really expect her to do couple-type things with him this weekend? That wasn't part of the deal. He'd said all she had to do was show up here so that Boyd Carter could see them together. Was he changing the rules on her now that they were here? And if so, what else might he expect of her?

As Elizabeth turned from the door, her gaze lit on the

four-poster. It was the kind of bed one could sink into, nestled in the arms of a lover….

She swallowed again as she turned back to Paul. He hadn't noticed that her attention had been caught by the bed, thank goodness. He was too busy picking up his suitcase and heading for the door. "I'll take the small bedroom. You'll be more comfortable in here."

"There's another bedroom? I didn't notice one."

"It's on the other side of the living room," Paul said. "The door was closed. That's probably why you didn't notice."

"But…how did you know it was there?" Elizabeth idly twisted a button at the top of her sweater. "No one said anything about two bedrooms."

He glanced away. "I've been up here before. I'm familiar with the layout."

He'd been up here before? Alone…or with a companion?

Elizabeth watched him leave the room. When she heard him moving about on the other side of the cottage, she opened the French doors wider and stepped out on the terrace.

The flagstones beneath her feet were slippery from the fog, and she took care as she walked about. The woods encroached to the very edge of the terrace, the giant, lacy firs casting a deep shadow over the space. It was colder out here, too, and the sound of the waterfall pounded an uneasy rhythm in the distance.

Elizabeth could see the trail they'd come up, and

where it led back into the trees, the mist thickened and swirled. For a moment the fog appeared to take on a human form, and then with a start Elizabeth realized that she really was seeing a man. He was walking toward the woods, but just before the shadows swallowed him, he turned. Elizabeth couldn't see his face, but she knew that he was looking at her. A chill slid over her, and she quickly went inside and locked the door.

After hanging her clothes in the roomy closet, she carried her toiletries into the bathroom, a luxurious, marble affair with a claw-foot tub large enough to accommodate two.

A bath sounded like a wonderful idea, Elizabeth decided. She sat on the edge of the tub as she turned on the taps. The hotel had supplied a generous cache of bath salts and spa treatments, and as she dumped some into the running water, the fragrance floated on the air like a dream.

She lit some candles, then quickly shed her clothing. Sinking down into the steamy bubbles, she lay her head back against the tub and let her muscles completely relax. She was only a blink away from dozing off when the room suddenly chilled. The candles flickered in the draft, and she sat up in alarm.

"Paul?" she called nervously. "Is that you?"

He didn't answer, but Elizabeth decided he must have gone out to the terrace for a breath of fresh air. How else to explain the draft?

Still, she couldn't shake her uneasiness, and climbing out of the tub, she quickly dried off and wrapped herself in a thick terry-cloth robe. Tying the sash, she walked into the bedroom and checked the terrace doors. They were still closed and locked, and as she moved into the living room, she could see nothing amiss there either.

Paul's door was ajar, and she went over to knock, but then noticed that he was stretched out on his bed asleep. He looked so peaceful, she hesitated to wake him. One leg hung off the side of the bed, and an arm was thrown over his face to shield it from the grayish light that filtered through the window. He appeared to be asleep, but as Elizabeth watched, he stirred and dropped his arm to his side. Rather than rousing, he seemed to settle more deeply into his slumber.

Elizabeth wasn't quite sure why she did it, but she crossed the room and dropped to her knees beside the bed. Resting her chin on her folded arms, she watched him sleep.

He had become a stranger to her, and yet his features were still so familiar. The thick, sweeping lashes she'd always envied. The well-shaped nose. The chiseled lips that still had the power to make her heart race.

For a moment she was overcome with the irresistible urge to lean over and press her mouth to those lips. She even moved her head toward him, and then that strange draft blew through the cottage again.

Getting to her feet, Elizabeth walked away from the bed to investigate. As she left Paul's room, his cell phone began to ring. She paused just outside his door, knowing that she shouldn't listen but unable to help herself.

She heard the bedsprings creak as he rolled over and reached for the phone. "Hello?" he said sleepily. He listened for a moment. "We got in a little while ago. Where are you?"

Another silence. Then he said, "No, it's best if you stay where you are. I'll see you in a little while."

He hung up and Elizabeth hurried back to her own bedroom, the source of the draft all but forgotten.

She had something else on her mind now—like who had been on the other end of Paul's phone conversation. She had a funny feeling that she already knew.

PAUL COULDN'T BELIEVE he'd slept so long. He'd only meant to lie down for a few moments to rest, and then the next thing he knew, he'd awakened to the scent of Elizabeth's perfume. He'd been dreaming about her, he supposed. Imagining that she had come to him the way she used to, soft and warm and fragrant from her bath. Her blue eyes dark and hooded with desire as she reached for him…

Getting up, he stretched, then glanced at his watch. He had fifteen minutes to shower and dress before the welcome cocktail party got under way in one of the small ballrooms. If he was late, he doubted anyone would notice. On the other hand, Boyd Carter valued promptness almost as much as he did family.

Wincing at the way Carter had him jumping through

hoops, Paul went in to take his shower. He emerged a few minutes later and quickly dressed in a dark suit and silk tie. Then he crossed the living room to check on Elizabeth.

Her door was open, and he could see her standing at the French doors, staring out into the darkness. Instead of knocking, Paul hovered on the threshold watching her. He could see her reflection in the glass and thought with a catch in his chest that she was as beautiful now as she had been thirteen years ago when they'd first met.

She'd been a typical University of Chicago college girl with her torn jeans and sneakers. She'd worn her hair natural back then, all curly and disheveled and hanging to her waist. It wasn't until she'd zeroed in on fashion design as a career that she'd cut her hair and transformed herself from an unkempt coed to the hip, sophisticated young woman she still was today.

She'd used a straightener on her hair, and it hung like a glossy curtain about her shoulders. The style was sleek and glamorous, but Paul still preferred all those wild curls. He'd never told her that, though. She was beautiful however she wore her hair.

The dress she had on was a simple black sheath that followed the narrow column of her figure, clinging subtly to her curves and dropping to just below her knees. Her feet were encased in the high heels she favored. The look was elegant, understated and sexy.

She turned and jumped when she saw him. Her hand flew to her throat. "Paul! I didn't see you there."

"Sorry. I…wanted to know if you're ready to go."

"Almost. I just have to put on my necklace." She walked over to the dresser and picked up a strand of pearls.

Paul couldn't seem to tear his gaze from her. The way she looked, the way she moved…how would he ever get over her?

She lifted the pearls to her neck and struggled for a moment with the clasp. Looking up, she said almost regretfully, "Do you mind?"

"No, of course, not." He walked over and took the necklace from her as she swept back her hair.

He'd forgotten how enticing the back of a woman's neck could be. Especially Elizabeth's. Her skin was pale and unblemished. As smooth as silk.

His fingers brushed against that creamy skin as he finally managed to get the necklace fastened. The ornate clasp was adorned with a tiny pearl and the engraved initial of the famous maker, and Paul remembered that he'd given the strand to Elizabeth for Christmas the year he'd made partner at the firm. She'd cried when she'd opened the velvet box, and her reaction had almost brought him to tears.

"Got it," he finally said, and Elizabeth stepped quickly away from him, letting her hair fall back into place.

"Now I'm ready," she said briskly as she picked up her wrap and evening bag from the bed, then walked over and grabbed her key from the nightstand. "Just in case I want to come back before you do," she explained, slipping the key into her purse.

They walked out together. Paul made sure the door was locked and then they headed down the walkway toward the hotel. It wasn't far. He could see the lights blazing from the arched windows just ahead, but the paved walkway was slippery and not all that smooth.

He glanced down at Elizabeth's heels. "Can you make it okay in those?"

"I've been wearing heels for years," she said airily. "I'll be fine—"

At that exact moment her heel caught on something and she stumbled. Paul grabbed her arm to steady her and suddenly they were standing face-to-face in the moonlight, cocooned in soft mist and silky darkness.

Her eyes were like cool, liquid crystals. They were the most beautiful eyes Paul had ever stared into, and for a moment he could have sworn he saw something— an invitation—in those glimmering depths.

He moved his head ever so slightly toward hers, and she stiffened, as if reading his intention in his eyes. "We should probably go. You don't want to be late."

The moment lost, Paul dropped his hand from her arm. "Yes, you're probably right." They walked along in silence the rest of the way. As they neared the terrace, he said, "So is Frankie coming up this weekend?"

"Yes, I think she planned to drive up late this afternoon. I don't know if she's here yet, though. I haven't talked to her."

"I'm surprised you both could get away from the shop this weekend," Paul said.

Elizabeth slanted him a glance. "Worried about your investment?"

"No, not at all."

They were nearing the pool area now. Paul could tell that the water was heated by the steam rising from the surface. The bluish glow from the underwater lights shimmered eerily on the undulating vapor.

"Paul…"

"Yes?"

She paused. "Regardless of what happens between us…it won't have any bearing on the agreement you have with the shop, will it?"

"Why would it?"

She drew her shawl more tightly around her, as if suddenly chilled. "Frankie is a little concerned that you might try to call in the loan."

He cocked his head slightly. "And what do you think?"

"I think you're an honorable man. You wouldn't do something like that."

"Did you tell her that?"

"Of course I did. But she doesn't know you like I do."

At least she still had some faith in him, Paul thought grimly. He wanted to take comfort in her defense of his honor, but the very fact that she'd brought up her partner's concerns meant that she wasn't quite as sure of his intentions as she tried to let on.

"I have no desire to call in the loan," he said coolly. "Why would I? If I let the interest accrue, I stand to make a killing."

Elizabeth bit her lip. "Maybe, if you'd charged the going rate. But you gave us very generous terms, and I want you to know that I appreciate everything you've done for us. We both do. It's just that…"

"Frankie doesn't know me the way you do," he repeated. He gazed down at her in the ghostly light. "Did it ever occur to you that you might not know Frankie as well as you think you do?"

Elizabeth frowned. "What do you mean by that?"

"She's very good at marketing your designs. I'll give her that. The deal with Nordstrom was a masterstroke. But when it comes to accounting matters, I think you'd be wise to keep a firm hold on the purse strings."

He started to turn back to the hotel, but Elizabeth grabbed his arm to stop him. "You can't just drop a bomb and walk away like that. What did you mean by that, Paul? Do you know something I don't?"

He hesitated. He'd wanted to talk to her about a concern he had with her partner for some time now, but he'd never found the right moment. They barely spoke two words to each other these days, and Paul had a feeling that Elizabeth wouldn't appreciate his meddling into her business affairs, even if his intentions were honorable. "My accountant found some discrepancies in the financial statements Frankie put together before we signed the loan agreement. I've been meaning to talk to you about it."

"What kind of discrepancies?" Elizabeth asked anxiously.

Paul glanced around as music and laughter drifted through the open terrace doors. "This isn't the time or place to get into it. We'll talk about it when we get back to Seattle."

"Paul—"

He put his hands on her shoulders. "It's probably nothing. I'm sure Frankie has a good explanation, but until we know for sure…watch yourself, okay? Especially if you're serious about dissolving the partnership. Take my advice and hire yourself a good attorney, because I guarantee you Frankie will be looking out for her own best interests."

Chapter Five

Elizabeth found it ironic that Paul had warned her about her partner in much the same way that Frankie had cautioned her about him. Apparently neither of them trusted her to look out for herself. Elizabeth supposed that was only to be expected after her erratic behavior of the past eighteen months and she tried not to resent their advice.

As soon as she and Paul entered the room, he was swept up in a conversation with several of his colleagues. Excusing herself, Elizabeth walked around the room searching for a spot where she might make herself as inconspicuous as possible. She found an alcove near the bar and settled in to watch the crowd. After a while she grew restless. She hadn't realized that she'd been searching for Paul until she finally spotted him again. He had his back to her, but she knew it was him, even from across the room.

He was still talking to the same circle of acquaintances that had drawn him in earlier, but now a woman stood at his side. As she turned to say something to Paul, Elizabeth caught her breath. It was Nina Wilson.

She looked ravishing in a vivid green dress that complemented her hair and molded to her womanly curves. As Elizabeth stood watching, Nina put her hand on Paul's arm, and he leaned down to hear what she had to say. It was a familiar, intimate gesture that made Elizabeth's heart pound in agitation.

She couldn't look away, and as if sensing the power of her stare, Nina scanned the crowd. As her gaze met Elizabeth's, she looked momentarily surprised and then she smiled.

She turned back to Paul and said something else that made them both laugh.

Angry and humiliated, Elizabeth hunted for the nearest exit. Finding an open French door, she hurried out to the terrace, her eyes burning with tears. She leaned against a column and gulped in cool air.

How dare he? How dare he bring that woman here? How dare he have the nerve to ask Elizabeth to come as a favor to him when he probably knew all along that Nina Wilson would be here, too?

Elizabeth still didn't understand why the prospect of Paul's infidelity mattered so much to her now that they were divorcing, but it did. It mattered terribly.

"I'm not the only one who doesn't like crowds, I see," a voice said from the darkness.

Elizabeth spun. She'd been so caught up in her righteous indignation that she hadn't noticed anyone else on the terrace. She still couldn't see him. Not at first. Then the mist swirled a bit as he stepped out of the shadows, a tall, broad-shouldered man dressed all in black.

A fist of fear tightened around Elizabeth's heart as she stared at him. He was a big man, and they were all alone out here. And there was something…unsettling about the way he had appeared.

Taking a deep breath, she finally found her voice. "I didn't know anyone else was out here. I'm sorry if I intruded on your solitude."

"An intrusion that I welcome," he said in a deep, fluid voice. "I've had enough seclusion to last me an eternity."

Chill bumps rose on the back of Elizabeth's neck. His voice was like a cold, dark river. "In that case, I'm surprised you don't like crowds," she tried to say lightly.

"It isn't a crowd of strangers that can alleviate loneliness, but the company of someone special."

He came out of the shadows then, and Elizabeth saw his face for the first time. He was older than Paul, probably around forty, and not nearly as handsome. But there was something compelling about his aristocratic features. High cheekbones and a long, patrician nose. A chiseled jaw and thick, black hair swept back from a wide, noble brow. His eyes were what held Elizabeth's attention, though. They were dark and glittering, like a pair of black diamonds.

As his gaze burned into hers, Elizabeth was surprised to feel a flutter of attraction in her stomach.

She glanced over her shoulder at the terrace doorway. "I should probably go back inside."

"No, don't run away." His voice was softly coercive. "You don't have to be afraid of me."

"I'm not afraid of you," Elizabeth denied.

"You are a little." He gave her a knowing smile. "But that will pass."

"Look, I don't..." Elizabeth wasn't certain what she'd been about to say. Her own thoughts seemed foreign to her at the moment. How could she be attracted to another man? Hadn't she just mentally berated Paul for inviting Nina Wilson up here for the weekend?

"Do I know you?" she asked hesitantly. "You seem...familiar to me." She winced as she said it. It sounded like the worst kind of come-on line.

But the stranger merely shrugged. "We've never met, but I have seen you."

"Where?" For some reason Elizabeth thought of all those times back in Seattle when she'd felt someone watching her. Her heartbeat quickened as he took a step toward her. Was it possible he'd followed her up here?

"I saw you when you arrived earlier today," he explained. "I was out strolling about the grounds."

Elizabeth remembered the feeling she'd had on the front steps of wanting to pull away from Paul, as if someone had been *compelling* her to pull away. But that was ridiculous. She was letting her imagination run away with her. And she'd been standing out here talking to a stranger long enough.

"I really should get back in. It's been nice talking to you, Mr..."

"Latimer. Roland Latimer III."

He moved even closer then, and Elizabeth let out a quick breath. It frosted on the night air. Funny, she hadn't thought it that cold, but suddenly she was shivering. She drew her shawl tightly around her shoulders. "How do you do, Mr. Latimer?"

"Roland, please." He reached for her hand, holding her so lightly that Elizabeth could barely feel him as he drew her palm to his mouth. His lips were as cool and soft as the mist, but when he lifted his gaze, Elizabeth saw flames of desire in those black eyes.

She quickly pulled her hand away.

"Elizabeth, is that you?" someone called behind her.

She whirled in relief. "Frankie!"

"I've been looking for you all evening," her partner said accusingly. "Where on earth have you been?"

"I'm glad you made it." Elizabeth sounded breathless and excited, although she wasn't quite sure why.

Frankie searched her face. "What are you doing out here? Are you okay?"

"Yes, of course."

Frankie glanced around the terrace. "Who were you talking to just now?"

"Oh, I'm sorry. Frankie, I'd like you to meet Mr. Latimer—" She turned. No one was there.

"Mr. who?"

Elizabeth glanced about the terrace. "He was here a minute ago. You must have seen him when you came out."

"I didn't see anyone," Frankie said. "I thought you were talking to yourself."

"Talking to myself? Why would you think that?" Elizabeth demanded.

Frankie hesitated. "I saw Paul with that woman inside. I figured you'd come out here to let off some steam."

Elizabeth turned back to the shadows, searching. "Her name is Nina Wilson," she said absently. "She's Paul's assistant."

"So?"

Elizabeth shrugged. "So maybe we were wrong about the situation at the restaurant."

"Because, God knows, no man has ever had an affair with his assistant," Frankie said snidely.

"That was uncalled for," Elizabeth said with a quick stab of anger.

"You're right. I was out of line." Frankie put a hand on Elizabeth's arm. "I'm sorry. It's just…I'm worried about you. You're not yourself. Like right now. You seem so distracted."

"I just asked my husband for a divorce," Elizabeth said bitterly. "I think I'm entitled to be a little distracted."

"Of course you are. I just don't want you to—"

"Go off the deep end again?" Elizabeth's mouth tightened. "That's what you're getting at, isn't it?"

Frankie sighed. "No, it's not. I don't want to see Paul take advantage of you, that's all."

"He won't."

"I know you think you can trust him because of your history together, but people change. Especially people going through a divorce."

Elizabeth had always tried to keep her personal and professional lives separate, but she hadn't realized until tonight how very little regard her business partner and her husband seemed to have for one another. She couldn't help wondering why.

"Lizzy…" Frankie glanced over her shoulder as someone came out on the terrace. She took Elizabeth's arm and pulled her toward the shadows. "Did you know that Dr. Summers is here?"

Elizabeth stared at her in shock. "*My* Dr. Summers?"

Frankie nodded. "I saw him a little while ago."

"But…how do you know it was him?" Elizabeth frowned. "You've never met him, have you?"

"No, but I was with a group of people at the bar and we all introduced ourselves. He said his name was Julian Summers, and then someone called him Dr. Summers. Tall, blond, very good-looking?"

"It sounds like him," Elizabeth admitted reluctantly.

Frankie looked anxious. "Why do you suppose he's here?"

"I have no idea." Elizabeth had gone to her therapist's office two days ago for a session. She'd told him all about her weekend plans with Paul. He'd been given the perfect opportunity to mention that he was coming up here, too. But he hadn't said a word, and now Elizabeth felt oddly betrayed.

"After I found out who he was, I kept my eye on him," Frankie said in a hushed tone. "I saw him talking to Paul."

Elizabeth bit her lip. She didn't want to hear any more of this, but she couldn't seem to resist questioning Frankie. "What did he say?"

"I don't know. I wasn't close enough to overhear the conversation, but they seemed pretty intense." Frankie paused. "I don't want to worry you, but there's something about this whole setup that bothers me. Think about it. Paul gets you up here on some lame pretext, and then we find out that his mistress—"

"We don't know that she's his mistress."

Frankie rolled her eyes. "True. We haven't caught them in bed...yet. Okay, we find out that his *assistant* and your therapist are also up here."

"It could be just a coincidence," Elizabeth insisted.

"Do you really believe that?" Frankie gave her a strange look. "Paul is the one who found Dr. Summers for you, isn't he?"

"Yes, why?"

"Because I guess I have to wonder, if push came to shove in a divorce settlement, which one of you would have his loyalty."

Elizabeth gazed at her in astonishment. "If you're suggesting that Paul would somehow try to use Dr. Summers against me, then you're even crazier than I am."

"Maybe I am crazy." Frankie shrugged. "But I don't think so. A man like Paul is used to getting what he wants and he's not afraid to pull out all the stops. He may have been a good guy in the past, but who's to say he doesn't have a dangerous side? A vindictive side? So watch yourself, okay?" She glanced uneasily over her shoulder. "And for God's sake, be careful."

INSTEAD OF RETURNING to the party, Elizabeth headed back to the cottage, where she could be alone. Paul would probably wonder where she'd gone off to, but she had no desire to go back inside and see him with Nina Wilson.

Undressing and slipping into her nightgown, Elizabeth crawled into bed and pulled the downy covers up to her chin. The room was warm enough, but she couldn't seem to stop shaking. She didn't think she would be able to sleep, but almost instantly she grew drowsy. The next thing she knew, she heard the door to the guest cottage open and close softly when Paul returned from the party.

Raising herself on her elbows, she called out to him. "Paul? Is that you?"

He came into her room then, looking young and movie-star handsome in his dark evening suit. He'd turned a lamp on in the other room, and as he stood backlit in the doorway, Elizabeth could see mist glistening in his hair. "Why did you leave without telling me?" he asked worriedly.

"I...had a headache. I decided to come back here and rest. I would have told you, but you were busy. I didn't want to bother you."

He came over to the foot of the bed, gazing down at her in concern. "Are you feeling better?"

"Yes, much better. Thanks."

"I tried to find you earlier," he said. "We didn't get a chance to eat before the party. I wondered if you wanted to have a late dinner."

"I'm not hungry—" Her stomach growled loudly, belying her claim, and she knew that Paul had heard it, too. She gave him a contrite look. "I guess I am hungry."

He smiled. "Good. We'll order room service." He turned and strode into the other room. When he came back, he sat down on the edge of the bed and handed her the menu. "What'll you have?"

She took a moment to study the choices. "I can't believe they actually have homemade chicken-noodle soup. My mother used to make it for me when I was a kid."

Paul lifted a brow. "You want chicken-noodle soup at a five-star hotel?"

Elizabeth shrugged. "Why not? It's comfort food."

He looked as if he wanted to ask her why she needed comfort, but instead he said, "How about a salad or sandwich to go along with it?"

Elizabeth folded the menu and handed it back to him. "Whatever you're having. I don't care."

She reached for her robe, but he said quickly, "No, don't get up. I'll call you when the food gets here."

He left the room then, and Elizabeth snuggled back under the covers. She had almost drifted off again when she heard a discreet knock on the door followed by the low rumble of voices. Climbing out of bed, she went to wash her face in the bathroom. Then, belting her robe around her, she joined Paul in the living room.

He had the table all set and had even lit a fire. The crackling flames set shadows to dancing along the walls and ceiling, making the room seem cozy and mysterious at the same time. Elizabeth watched as he added another log to the blaze.

He'd changed into jeans and a sweater, and as he bent to his work, Elizabeth thought he'd never looked more handsome than with firelight dancing across his features.

"Still hungry?" he asked over his shoulder.

"Yes, I'm starving."

"Good. Let's eat then."

They sat down at the table and removed the stainless-steel tops from the dishes. The soup was still steaming and Elizabeth let it cool for a moment before she took her first taste.

"Delicious," she said with a sigh.

"I'm glad to see that you've gotten your appetite back," Paul said with a smile.

"I haven't exactly been wasting away," Elizabeth replied as she spooned another mouthful.

"You're still very thin." He gave her a worried look.

"I have to be thin to fit into my own designs," she said lightly.

"The dress you had on tonight…was that one of yours?"

"No, I got it off the sale rack at Nordstrom. Why?"

"I liked it," Paul said. "You looked…nice tonight."

"So did you."

He seemed surprised and pleased by the compliment. "Thanks."

Elizabeth put down her spoon. "I guess I'm not the only one who noticed."

He glanced up curiously.

"I'm talking about your assistant, Nina Wilson. She seemed very attentive tonight," Elizabeth said.

Paul frowned. "What are you getting at?"

"I think you know." She searched his face for a guilty flicker in his eyes, a telltale twitch of a muscle in his cheek, but there was nothing. Just his unrelenting stare.

He laid aside his own silverware. "If you've got something on your mind, then just say it outright."

"Are you having an affair with her?" Elizabeth blurted.

He looked stunned, then his features went tight with anger. "Why the hell would you ask me that?"

Elizabeth tried to swallow past the bad taste that rose in her mouth. The thought of Paul and another woman…she still couldn't bear it.

Closing her eyes briefly, she summoned up her courage. She'd started this. Now she had to see it through. "I saw the two of you together at a restaurant the other day. She looked very attentive then, too."

"You saw us at a restaurant so you jumped to the conclusion that we're having an affair? God, Elizabeth." He raked his fingers through his dark hair. "You must not have a shred of faith in me anymore." He shoved back his chair and stalked over to the fireplace.

Elizabeth clasped her trembling hands in her lap. "It wasn't just the fact that the two of you were together at the restaurant. I saw her in the bathroom. She didn't know who I was, but she said something that made me think that she's in love with you. She is, isn't she? That woman is in love with you."

She could almost see the denial forming on his lips, then he glanced down at the blaze. "Okay, yes. I think she may have feelings for me. But I swear, I didn't know it until tonight." He looked up from the fire, his expression earnest. "I didn't invite her up here, Elizabeth. She just showed up."

Elizabeth's heart had already been pounding, but now it slammed against her chest. "What do you mean?"

"Just what I said. I was as surprised to see her here as you were."

"But…you were talking to her," Elizabeth said. "Laughing with her. You didn't look as if you minded that she was here at all."

"She came up to me while I was involved in a conversation with Boyd Carter and some of the other investors. I didn't want to create a scene, and she knew it. She took advantage of the situation."

"And that's all there is to it?"

His gaze met hers. "Yes. That's all there is to it. I'm not having an affair. Not with Nina Wilson or anyone else. There's never been anyone but you since the moment I first laid eyes on you."

Elizabeth glanced down. "You don't have to say that."

"Why not? It's true."

"Paul—"

"As long as we're clearing the air, there's something I want to get straight with you, too." He paused. "I don't want this divorce."

Panic prickled along Elizabeth's backbone. "But you said—"

"I said when we get back you can file for divorce and I won't try to stop you. I meant that. But it's not what I want."

He came back over to the table then. Bending, he put his hands on her arms and pulled her up so that he could search her face as he spoke. "I'm still in love with you, Elizabeth. And I think somewhere deep inside, you still love me, too."

"But I already told you that," she said desperately. Her heartbeat drummed in her ears. "I do love you, Paul. But it's not enough anymore. It's not—"

"Passionate love? I think it is," he said softly. "Or it could be. I think the passion is still there. We just have to find it."

"But I don't want to find it," Elizabeth whispered. "I just…"

"What do you want? Tell me."

She glanced away. "I just want to be left alone."

Instead of releasing her, he tightened his grasp on her

arms. "Yes, I know. You've made that abundantly clear. But I let you go once. I let you push me away. I'm not going to make that same mistake again."

"But it's over!" she said fiercely.

He shook his head, his gray eyes calm and resolved. "It's not over. Not until the end of this weekend. Not until we get back to Seattle."

"That's ridiculous. We can't repair the damage to our marriage in the space of one weekend. Besides, that's not even why we came up here." She watched his eyes and gasped. "You tricked me into coming up here, didn't you?" When he didn't deny it, she said angrily, "What about Boyd Carter?"

"I don't give a damn about Boyd Carter. You're the only one I care about. You're the only thing in my life that means anything to me."

His hands slid up her arms and suddenly he was cupping her face in his hands as she gazed up at him. "Remember the way it used to be, Elizabeth? The way you used to tremble when we kissed?"

"Don't—"

But it was too late. He'd already claimed her lips. He was gentle at first and then, when she didn't resist, he deepened the kiss with his tongue.

He kissed her as he hadn't kissed her in years, and an electric thrill shot through Elizabeth's body. She put her hands on his chest, to shove him away at first and then to cling to his shirt as her knees grew weak.

Threading his fingers through her hair, he pulled

back for a moment to stare into her eyes. Then he kissed her again and kept on kissing her until the ringing of his cell phone caused them to jerk apart.

Paul swore.

"You'd better get it." Elizabeth put quivering fingers to her lips. "It could be important."

He gave her a look that told her he knew exactly what she was doing, then he turned and strode over to the end table where he'd left his phone. Glancing at the caller ID, his features hardened as he jerked the phone to his ear. "What do you want, Nina?" His gaze met Elizabeth's. A fury she'd never seen before glimmered in those dark depths, making her tremble even harder. She'd never seen Paul so angry.

"No, you listen to me," he said coldly. "I want you out of here first thing in the morning. Go back to Seattle and clean out your office. I'll have Accounting cut you a severance check on Monday."

He hung up then, his gaze still on Elizabeth. "Does that answer your previous question?"

"If it was really Nina on the phone." Elizabeth had no idea why she said that. It wasn't like her. She wasn't normally a suspicious or vindictive person, but suddenly she couldn't help herself. She couldn't…stop herself.

Paul approached her slowly, his eyes going colder than Elizabeth had ever seen them. "Why did you say that?"

She shrugged. "A phone conversation doesn't prove anything, does it?"

"You still believe I'm having an affair? After every-

thing I just said to you. After the way we just kissed."
His expression turned derisive. "Maybe you're right.
Maybe what we had *is* gone. Because the Elizabeth I
knew was never this distrustful."

"And the Paul I knew wouldn't look at me as if he
expects me to go off the deep end at any moment," Elizabeth countered. "Living with you is like living in a
goldfish bowl. You watch me constantly. Do you have
any idea how unnerving that is?"

He gazed at her in disbelief. "I've got good reason
to be concerned about you. Or have you forgotten?"

"I haven't forgotten anything. One kiss can't make
me forget the past eighteen months, Paul. I still want a
divorce."

He turned away, as if he couldn't bear to look at her.

Elizabeth drew a breath. "And while we're still clearing the air, there's something else I need to know."

He didn't turn, but stood with his back to her.
"What?"

"Did you ask Dr. Summers to come up here this
weekend?"

He faced her slowly. "Dr. Summers? Why on earth
would you think that?"

"Because why else would he be here?" Elizabeth
demanded.

"There must be over a hundred people here this weekend. I'm the only one who could have invited him?"

"You're saying his being here is just a coincidence?"

"I'm saying you're not his only patient. For your information, Annika Wallenburg was the one who recommended him. She's been taking her grandmother to see him for years."

Something crumpled in Elizabeth's stomach. "He's here to see Mrs. Wallenburg?"

"I don't know why he's here," Paul said. "But I can assure you I'm not the reason."

"Then I apologize."

"For what? Accusing me of being an adulterer and a liar? Apology accepted." He gave her a disgusted look. "If the interrogation is over, I'm going to bed."

He stalked out of the room and slammed his bedroom door.

Elizabeth stood trembling in the living room. Why had she done that? Why had she provoked him that way? She'd never been the confrontational type, but all of a sudden it was as if she'd wanted to hurt him. She'd wanted to push him away. She'd wanted to drive a stake through the heart of their marriage so there would be no turning back. No second-guessing her decision.

Why?

Because he was getting to her?

PAUL TOSSED AND TURNED. He couldn't find a comfortable position, probably because he didn't feel the least bit sleepy. Finally giving up, he rolled over and had just reached for the light when he heard a low moan from Elizabeth's room. He recognized it. He'd heard the sound often enough in the past year and half. She was in the throes of a nightmare.

Shoving back the covers, he got up and walked barefoot through the living room to Elizabeth's door. He started to knock, but he knew from past experience that she probably wouldn't hear him. He'd have to go in and gently shake her awake.

He tried the door and assumed when it didn't open that she'd locked it from the inside. He pushed again and this time it flew open with such force, the knob was snatched from his hand.

The draft sweeping in through the open terrace door struck him like a physical blow. It was freezing inside her room. Paul stood on the threshold, momentarily paralyzed by the cold. Fog had crept in, too, and now it hovered over her bed, writhing in the wind.

There was something strange about that mist. For a moment it almost seemed to Paul—

He wouldn't even allow himself to finish the thought. Reaching for the switch, he turned on a lamp. The vapor instantly disappeared in the light. He hurried over and shut the terrace door, making sure to engage the lock.

Elizabeth didn't stir, but her moaning stopped the moment he closed the door. He went over to sit on the edge of her bed, wondering if he should still wake her up.

He was reaching to touch her arm when her eyes flew open and she bolted upright in bed. "He's here," she said in a strange, breathy voice. "He's in my room."

"It's okay," Paul said quickly. "It's just me."

She stared at him, but it was almost as if she didn't see him. Then she visibly started. Her hand flew to her heart, and she had to struggle to catch her breath.

"I'm sorry," Paul said. "I didn't mean to scare you. You were having a nightmare."

She blinked, as if trying to bring him into focus. "A nightmare?"

"Yes. I heard you from my room. I came in to check on you."

She eased herself back against the pillows and pulled up the blanket. "It was just a nightmare." She squeezed her eyes closed.

"Do you want to talk about it?"

She cringed and seemed to shrink even deeper under the cover. "I was in this…awful place. It was cold and dark. Like a grave."

A shiver snaked up Paul's spine. "It was just a dream."

She didn't seem to hear him. "I couldn't get out. I heard you calling to me, but…I knew you wouldn't be able to find me. Not in time. And I couldn't…I couldn't get to you. And then *he* was there."

"Who?"

"Roland Latimer."

Paul frowned. "Do I know him?"

"I thought you might," Elizabeth said almost hopefully. "I met him at the party tonight. I went outside for some air and he…just sort of appeared out of nowhere."

"What do you mean?"

"He was standing in the shadows. I didn't see him at first. Then he started talking to me, and I guess…he frightened me a little. That's why I dreamed about him."

Paul didn't like what he was hearing one bit. "What did he say to you, Elizabeth? Did he threaten you?"

"No, no, it wasn't like that. He didn't say much of anything. We only spoke for a minute or two, and then when Frankie came outside, he…disappeared. She thought I was talking to myself," Elizabeth said with a shaky laugh. "Crazy, huh?" Her gaze met Paul's. "He was there, though. I didn't make him up."

"I never thought you did." He got up and went over to check outside her window. "I've never heard of him, but I'll see if I can find out who he is tomorrow. I'll make sure he doesn't bother you again."

"No, don't do that. He really didn't say or do anything out of line. If you confront him, you'll just embarrass us all. Please, Paul. Let it go."

He came back over to the bed. "If that's what you want."

"It is."

He could see that she was still disturbed, though. And it certainly wouldn't hurt to find out a little more about this Roland Latimer. Just to be on the safe side.

He tucked the covers around her shoulders. "You're still shaking."

"I guess I have a chill."

"No wonder. You left the terrace door open before you went to sleep. The room was like a meat locker when I came in."

"I didn't leave the door open," Elizabeth said uneasily. "I went out to get some air earlier, but I'm sure I closed it behind me."

"It was open when I came in. That's not a good idea. Especially with creeps like this Latimer guy hanging around."

Elizabeth clutched the blanket. "I don't think he means me any harm. He was just someone invited to the party. And anyway, I'm pretty sure I did close that door. It must have blown open."

"Well, in any case, it's closed now," Paul said. "And it's already getting warmer in here. Can you feel it?"

She nodded. "Yes. I feel much better. You don't have to stay with me. I'm fine now."

"I don't mind staying for a while. It usually takes you a while to get settled again after one of your nightmares."

"You don't have to do that," she said. "It's not your job to calm me down. I'm not your responsibility anymore."

"I'm not allowed to still care about you?" he asked softly.

Elizabeth glanced away. "Of course you are. And I'm glad you came. The nightmare…" She trailed off.

"It was a bad one."

"Yes." She sighed.

"Then let me stay for a while." He got up and walked over to the easy chair by the window. "I'll just sit here quiet as a church mouse. You won't even know I'm here."

Elizabeth shook her head, but she was smiling.

"What's wrong?" he asked as he sat down and made himself comfortable.

"I don't know. What you said about being quiet as a church mouse. It made me picture what you'd look like in one of those mouse hats from Disney World."

"I've always looked good in hats," he said lightly. "Even one with ears."

Elizabeth's laugh was like music to him. He was starved for the sound, but she almost instantly sobered. "Paul, about what I said earlier…"

"It's okay."

"No, it's not okay. I don't know why I said those things to you. I don't know what came over me. It was as if…I wanted to hurt you."

"You thought I was having an affair."

"I don't now."

"That's a relief."

"You're a good man, Paul," she whispered. "You've been a good husband."

He had a difficult time swallowing past the sudden lump in his throat. "It means a lot to hear you say that."

They were both silent for a long time, then Elizabeth said almost in exasperation, "For God's sake, you look so uncomfortable in that chair. Go back to your room and get some sleep. You probably have a busy day tomorrow."

"I have a meeting with Boyd Carter at two. I thought we could hike up to the waterfall before that if you feel up to it. No ulterior motive," he added quickly. "It's a beautiful spot. I thought you might like to see it."

"I would."

"Good. Then get some sleep."

"What about you?"

"I'm fine where I am for now." He reached over and turned out the light.

"Don't stay there all night," Elizabeth warned from the darkness.

"I won't. Just until you fall asleep."

She didn't say anything else, and after a few moments Paul could tell from the sound of her soft breathing that she'd fallen back asleep. He was surprised she'd dozed off so quickly. It sometimes took her hours to go back to sleep after a nightmare.

He was glad, though. She needed her rest. He was worried about her. Her earlier accusations had been disquieting enough, but now with the nightmare...

Paul was very much afraid that Elizabeth was still balanced on an emotional edge. He wondered if he should give Dr. Summers a call, but if the therapist had come up here to relax, Paul would be the last person he'd want to hear from. Their last conversation back in the city had ended in an argument, with Paul accusing him of trying to turn Elizabeth against him. He'd apologized for his temper, and Dr. Summers had promised not to mention the confrontation to Elizabeth. But Paul wasn't so sure how far he trusted Summers these days. It wouldn't be the first time a therapist fell for his patient.

Finally succumbing to exhaustion, Paul laid his head against the back of the chair, but every time he closed his eyes, the room seemed to grow chillier. It was only his imagination, of course, but something seemed to be warning him not to drift off.

Sitting up in the chair, he rubbed the sleep from his eyes and glanced out the terrace doors where the mist had thickened. It coiled and writhed against the glass, and for a moment it almost appeared to Paul that the vapor was trying to get back in.

He rubbed his eyes again.

Maybe he was the one who needed a shrink.

Chapter Six

Elizabeth had already made coffee by the time Paul got up the next morning. She was having her first cup when he came out of his room and she was stunned by his appearance. He always left for work earlier than she did, so their paths rarely crossed in the mornings. She'd forgotten how he looked all freshly shaved and hair still damp from his shower.

He was dressed as she was in jeans and a sweater, and on first glance he looked years younger than his age. Then she saw the dark circles under his eyes and winced.

"Did you get any sleep last night?"

"Enough." He came over and poured himself a cup of coffee. "How about you?"

"I was out like a light." Which was surprising. Normally she remained restless for hours after a nightmare. Maybe this place really did have therapeutic qualities, although Elizabeth had to wonder if her restful sleep had more to do with Paul's presence than anything else.

She gave him a guilty look. "You spent the night in that chair, didn't you? It can't have been very comfortable."

He shrugged as he sipped his coffee. "I fell asleep, so it couldn't have been that bad. I woke up just after dawn and moved into the other room."

"Thanks for waking me up last night," Elizabeth murmured. "And for staying with me. You really didn't have to do that."

"I didn't mind." He didn't seem to want to talk about it anymore. He carried his coffee over to the window and stared out. "What are your plans for the day?"

"I thought we were going to hike up to the waterfall."

He glanced over his shoulder. "You want to do that? It looks as if it might start raining any second now."

Elizabeth set aside her cup and stood. "We're Seattleites. A little rain can't stop us."

Her positive response seemed to surprise him. "Okay. If that's what you want. Better take a jacket, though. Something waterproof if you have one."

She went to retrieve her jacket and then they set out. Once they left the hotel grounds, the paved trail ended and became little more than a dirt path that led back into the woods.

In spite of the clouds, the scenery was breathtaking—a lush Jurassic forest of giant firs, moss and ferns. Elizabeth wouldn't have been surprised to see the water in the rocky creek bed quake from some distant dinosaur footfall.

As they neared the waterfall, the quiet was broken by

the sound of rushing water and the air became noticeably cooler. A fine mist descended over them as they topped an incline and stood on a rocky cliff.

A ten-foot scramble up another slippery rise would have put them at the summit. Elizabeth could see rocks forming a natural bridge across the crest of the waterfall, but to cross to the other side would be an extremely risky endeavor. When she moved to the edge of the bluff, she could look over and see the water crashing against giant boulders twenty feet down. She doubted anyone could survive a fall like that.

As she started to move back, her foot slipped on the damp moss. Paul's hand shot out to pull her away from the edge.

"Don't get too close," he warned. "It's slippery up here, and you almost gave me a heart attack."

"How about if I sit over here and watch from a distance?" Elizabeth walked over and sat down on a fallen log.

"Good idea," Paul agreed. He turned back to the water, and they both fell silent. Elizabeth didn't know why, but there was something deeply spiritual about the place. It was almost like being in a chapel.

After a while the sun came out, and in the dappled light that filtered through the lacy canopy, tiny rainbows danced across the water. Elizabeth took it as a sign.

And then she felt it. That familiar brush against her fingers.

She couldn't see him, of course. But he was there,

sitting on the log beside her. She could feel him. She closed her eyes and drank in his scent.

After a moment she checked to see if Paul had noticed, but his gaze was still on the rushing water.

A butterfly caress against her cheek and then he was gone.

She looked up to find Paul watching her strangely. "Are you okay?"

Elizabeth raised her hand to her cheek. "I was just…wishing that I'd brought my camera."

"We're not leaving until Tuesday. We'll have plenty of time to come back."

Today was Friday. They still had three more days of the long weekend to get through, but somehow those days didn't stretch out endlessly as they once had when Elizabeth had contemplated the trip. This spot, this time with Paul…

Things were changing between them. Her resolve was weakening, and their growing closeness made her apprehensive. What if their feelings weren't real but only a memory of what they'd once had? Did she really want to put herself through an emotional roller coaster to find out? She'd been through so much already. An agonizing decision had been made. It was too late to go back. It was time for both of them to move on.

And yet at that moment all she wanted to do was put her hand in Paul's and let him feel where their son had touched her. She desperately wanted that connection with him, but Paul wouldn't understand. How could he? Elizabeth didn't understand it herself. She didn't believe in ghosts. She knew her son's spirit hadn't touched her on the hand and kissed her cheek. It was only his memory.

Even so, as soon as Paul left that afternoon for his meeting with Boyd Carter, Elizabeth grabbed her camera and jacket and headed back to the waterfall.

The sun was still shining, but somehow the woods seemed more foreboding now, probably because she was alone. She topped the incline and stood on the cliff watching the pounding water. The temperature had dropped so low that even her jacket couldn't keep out the cold. Shivering, she waited and waited, but nothing happened. No brush against her fingers. No whisper-soft caress against her cheek.

As she stood huddled in her coat, she heard a strange cry and glanced skyward to see a vulture circling overhead. Another one came and then another. Soon there were dozens swooping down to settle in the trees all around her.

Elizabeth felt a chill like nothing she'd ever experienced before as she gazed up into those trees. It was almost as if the vultures were waiting for something—or someone—to die.

A twig snapped behind her and she whirled in shock. "What are you doing here?"

Nina Wilson shrugged as she brushed by Elizabeth to stand at the edge of the precipice. "Enjoying the scenery, same as you are."

Elizabeth moved away from her. "I thought you'd gone back to the city."

"Why would you think that?" Nina asked absently as she gazed down where the water beat against the boulders. She was dressed in jeans and a waterproof jacket with a hood that hid her flaming hair. Shoving her hands into the pockets of her jacket, she moved even closer to the edge.

"I heard Paul's phone conversation with you last night," Elizabeth said. "He told me everything."

Nina gave her a sidelong look. "Everything? Oh, I doubt that. Besides, I didn't talk to Paul after we left the party."

Elizabeth's heart began to knock against her chest. "You didn't call him on his cell phone?"

"Why should I when I knew I'd be seeing him later?" Nina turned then and smiled at Elizabeth. "I don't mean to be so blunt, but we might as well get everything out in the open, hadn't we? It's better for everyone."

"I already know that you're in love with my husband," Elizabeth said coldly.

"Did he tell you that?" Nina shrugged. "Okay, then, yes, I'm in love with Paul. And he loves me, too."

"I don't believe you."

She gave Elizabeth a pitying smile. "Well, you would have if you could have seen him with me last night." She reached out suddenly and touched her fingertip to the tiny diamond crescent Elizabeth wore at her throat. "Lovely," she murmured. "A present from Paul?"

A shudder ripped through Elizabeth, and she jerked away from the woman's touch. "You and Paul weren't together last night. He was with me. We had a late dinner."

Something flickered in Nina Wilson's green eyes. Anger, yes, but with it a hint of obsession. Elizabeth's gaze fell to the woman's hands. She'd shoved them back into her jacket pockets.

"And after you had dinner?"

"That's none of your business."

Nina laughed. "You can't pull it off, you know. You don't have the face for a bluff like that." Her expression turned sly. "You may have had a late dinner together, but what about afterward? You can't keep track of your husband's every move when you don't share the same bedroom with him."

Elizabeth stood frozen in shock. How could Nina have known that? Elizabeth had never confided the intimate details of her and Paul's relationship to anyone except Dr. Summers. And maybe Frankie. But no one else.

Not that it mattered. Their bedroom arrangement was no one else's business. What mattered was how the woman had found out. She couldn't have known unless Paul had told her.

No, that wasn't true. There were other ways for a clever woman like Nina to find out what she needed.

And she was clever. The shrewdness was there in her eyes, along with the obsession.

Elizabeth shivered. "Not that it's any of your concern, but as it happens, I do know my husband's where-abouts last evening. He was with me all night."

Anger flashed again in Nina's eyes, and her laugh now sounded brittle and forced. "You're lying. Paul hasn't slept with you in ages."

"Why don't we go ask him?" Elizabeth challenged. "I'd love to see my husband's reaction when he hears what you have to say."

"He would say and do anything to keep you ap-peased until a divorce settlement is reached," Nina countered as she turned back to the waterfall. "Don't you get that? Don't you get that Paul is through with you? He needs a real woman in his life and in his bed. Not some cold fish—"

As she said the last word, her feet slipped on the wet moss, and for a moment she hovered at the edge of the cliff, her arms flailing wildly.

And then Elizabeth grabbed her and pulled her to safety.

The woman spun, obviously shaken. She put a hand to her heart as she stared wild-eyed at Elizabeth. "What the hell is wrong with you? You almost killed me!"

Her words were like a physical blow. Elizabeth stum-bled back from her. "What are you talking about? You slipped and I grabbed you."

"You pushed me!" Nina's eyes were still wide with shock. "I felt your hand on my back."

"I didn't push you," Elizabeth whispered. "It wasn't me."

"Stop lying! We both know what happened." Nina brushed past Elizabeth then and stalked toward the path. Turning, she said over her shoulder, "Paul's right. You really are insane."

AFTER HIS MEETING WITH Boyd Carter, Paul headed for the lobby. He waited until the crowd had dispersed from around the front desk before approaching the clerk.

The man looked up with a friendly smile. "May I help you?"

"I hope so. I'm looking for someone—a man named Roland Latimer. Could you ring his room for me?"

"One moment, sir."

The clerk typed the name into the computer, waited a moment, then glanced up. "I'm afraid we don't have anyone registered by that name."

Paul frowned. "I know he's here. He was at the party last night."

The clerk shrugged apologetically. "I'm sorry, sir. There's no one registered by that name."

"Maybe he's an employee," Paul suggested.

"The name doesn't sound familiar to me." The desk clerk's smile faded as he grew a bit impatient. "And at any rate, I don't have access to employee records."

Paul's voice hardened as he leaned across the counter. "Then let me talk to someone who does. Immediately."

The man started to balk, then, sensing Paul's mood, nodded. "One moment."

He disappeared through a doorway behind the desk

and returned a few minutes later with a polished thirty-something woman with a no-nonsense smile and a name tag that identified her as an assistant manager.

"May I help you?" she asked briskly.

"I'm looking for a man named Roland Latimer. He was at the party last night, so I assume he's either a guest or an employee here at the hotel. I need to have a word with him."

A shadow flickered across the woman's face. She didn't strike him as the type of person to be easily intimidated, but he detected the barest hint of a nervous twitch at the corner of her left eye, as if he'd said something to upset her. "We show no record of anyone having registered under that name, nor is he an employee. The man you're looking for is probably a local."

"Really?" Paul wasn't convinced. "I was under the impression that everyone invited here this weekend is somehow connected to the hotel."

"Yes, most of our guests this weekend have an affiliation in one way or another to Fernhaven, but it's not unusual to have a gate-crasher at these events." She hesitated, as if not quite sure how to proceed. "I suggest you drive into the village and ask around about this man. The main highway will take you straight into Cedar Cove. You'll see a place on the right called the Front Street Diner. You can't miss it. A woman named Audrey Sylvester runs the place. From what I hear, she knows most everyone who lives around here. She should be able to help you."

Paul had a feeling the assistant manager was being purposefully evasive, but he also knew that it would be unproductive to try and coerce more information from her. He'd only alienate her, and he might need her help in the future if Latimer showed up at the hotel again.

Nodding his thanks, he left the lobby and had his car brought around. He was on the road in less than five minutes.

The tiny village of Cedar Cove was a thirty-minute drive from the hotel and accessible only by a bridge that had been badly damaged in a recent flood. The bridge had been repaired, but the water was still so high in places that the mist hovering over the surface crept through the metal guardrails, creating an odd, dizzying sensation as Paul drove across.

A sign on the side of the road warned him to decrease his speed as he approached the city limits. The two-lane highway turned into Front Street, and as he cruised along the shady thoroughfare, he searched for the diner. He'd almost driven past the weathered redbrick building before he spotted the words *Front Street Diner* painted in black across the plate-glass window. Finding a parking place on the street, he got out and backtracked to the diner.

A bell over the door announced his arrival, and the few patrons scattered about the tables stared at him openly as he walked over to the counter and took a seat on one of the old-fashioned stools.

A pretty blond waitress in a pink uniform hurried over

to pour him a cup of coffee. "Hi, I'm Katie," she greeted with a perky smile. "Would you like to see a menu?"

"No, coffee is fine."

"Are you coming or going?" she asked curiously.

"I beg your pardon?"

"Are you coming from or going up to the hotel?"

The question took Paul by surprise. "I just drove down, but how did you know that?"

"Just a guess." Her smiled turned appreciative as she gave him a quick once-over. "You're not from around here, that's for sure."

Ignoring her mild flirtation, Paul picked up his cup. "That's good coffee," he murmured after taking a sip.

"Coffee's our specialty," she said proudly. "We may not have the fancy lattes and cappuccinos they have in Seattle, but no one makes a better cup of java than Audrey."

He set down his cup. "Would that be Audrey Sylvester?"

The young woman's brows shot skyward. "How do you know Audrey?"

"I don't. But one of the managers at the hotel suggested that I talk to her. I'm trying to find someone who may live around here."

She nodded. "Audrey would be the person to talk to, all right. She knows everyone, and I do mean everyone, in town."

"Is she here?"

"She's always here," the waitress said with a resigned sigh. She glanced over to where an older woman dressed in an identical pink uniform appeared to be engaged in a heated conversation with a customer. "Hey, Audrey! This gentleman would like to have a word with you."

"Hold your horses, I'll be right there," came the grumpy reply.

The older waitress took another few minutes to finish up with the customer, then, throwing a dish towel over her shoulder, she strode toward Paul. She was a formidable-looking woman, tall, stout, with chopped-off hair and a scowling, put-upon demeanor. Judging from her dour expression, her philosophy wasn't that the customer was always right, but rather an annoyance that had to be dealt with.

"I'm Audrey Sylvester," she said as she tilted her head to get a better look at Paul through the huge glasses she wore perched on the end of her nose. "What can I do for you?"

"He's trying to find someone," Katie offered helpfully.

"Now was I talking to you?" Audrey demanded testily. Her cranky disposition was a stark counterpoint to the other woman's youthful verve. "And by the way, if you've finished admiring the scenery, why don't you see to your other customers? You don't get paid to stand around gawking at strangers."

Katie turned bright red and scurried off in dismay.

Oblivious—or more likely indifferent—to the younger woman's embarrassment, Audrey Sylvester leaned an arm against the counter as she continued to study Paul through her glasses. "So who did you say you're looking for?"

"A man named Roland Latimer. I was told you might know where I could find him."

Something flickered in Audrey's eyes, but before she could respond, a loud crash drew them around with a start. Katie had dropped a carafe of scalding coffee, and the glass had shattered against the tile floor. She didn't seem to notice the dark stain spreading toward a nearby table as she gazed at Paul in astonishment.

"Well, don't just stand there." Audrey threw the young woman a towel. "Get that mess cleaned up."

"Yes, ma'am." Her focus still on Paul, Katie hurried around the counter and headed for the kitchen door, muttering something about a broom and a mop. Taking one last glance at Paul, she pushed open the door and rushed through.

Paul turned back to Audrey. "What was that all about?"

Audrey shrugged. "She's still pretty green. You'll have to excuse her jitters."

Paul wasn't at all convinced that the young waitress's inexperience had caused her to drop the coffeepot. He had a feeling it had something to do with Roland Latimer.

"Do you know Roland Latimer?" he asked bluntly.

Audrey straightened and, grabbing a fresh towel, busily scrubbed at an invisible spot on the counter. "Nope, haven't had the pleasure. You might want to talk to Zoë Lindstrom, though. She's lived here a lot longer than I have. If anyone can help you, she can."

Why did he get the feeling that Audrey Sylvester, like the assistant manager at the hotel, was trying to get rid of him? Just who the hell was this Latimer guy? "Where can I find Ms. Lindstrom?"

"It's Miss, actually. She's never married. But anyway, she prefers Zoë. Her house is only a couple of blocks from here. When you go out the door, turn right and stay on Front Street for two blocks, then make another right on Tall Pines. About halfway down the street you'll see a white two-story house with a wrought-iron fence around the front yard. Kind of run-down looking. That's Zoë's place. You can't miss it."

"Should I call first?" Paul asked as he reached for his wallet.

"I'll give her a buzz and let her know you're on your way over."

"Thanks. I appreciate that." Paul started to toss some bills onto the table, but Audrey put up a hand to stop him.

"Coffee's on the house. If you liked it, spread the word. Maybe we'll get a little tourist business from the hotel."

"Thanks. I'll do that."

As Paul walked away from the diner he had the distinct feeling that he was being watched. Glancing over his shoulder, he saw the young waitress standing at the plate-glass window, staring after him, but when he turned, she darted away, as if not wanting to be spotted.

Something strange was going on around here, Paul decided. And that something obviously had to do with Roland Latimer.

Chapter Seven

No one was about. The silence was a little unnerving, Paul decided as he followed Audrey's directions. He wasn't used to such sluggish traffic on a Friday afternoon. By midday in Seattle the streets would already be clogged with commuters anxious to jump-start their weekend.

He'd once been just as eager to get home, but since the accident—since Elizabeth had frozen him out of her grief—he'd gotten into the habit of working late on Friday nights to avoid the traffic. By the time he left the office at around ten or eleven he mostly had to contend with the pedestrians that jammed the streets.

If he drove, he still tried to avoid the main arteries, but on the occasions when he walked home, he took his time, enjoying the excitement that thrummed through downtown.

Before Damon was born, he and Elizabeth had taken full advantage of the Seattle nightlife. Their Belltown condo was only minutes away from some of the hottest nightclubs in the city. Another few blocks and they had their pick of restaurants and bars along the waterfront.

Nowadays Paul usually came home to a dark apartment. Elizabeth made a point of turning in early, but he'd often see a light underneath her door which he took to mean she was still awake. He used to knock softly to check on her, but she'd come to resent the intrusion, so he'd stopped. He shouldn't have, he realized now. He shouldn't have let her push him away.

Turning down Tall Pines, he spotted the house Audrey had described, and pausing outside the wrought-iron gate, he glanced around as a strange uneasiness gripped him.

The house disturbed him. He couldn't explain it. The structure itself was quaint and charming with its bay windows and wraparound shape. The architecture was reminiscent of some of the older neighborhoods in Seattle, but unlike most of those homes, this one hadn't been recently renovated. The paint was peeling and the porch sagged at one end. But it wasn't the overall deterioration of the place that sent a chill up Paul's spine. Nor was it the sudden drop in temperature as he opened the gate and stepped into the deeply shaded front yard.

Something *inside* the house made him want to turn and hurry away without looking back.

Which was crazy, Paul chided himself. He hadn't even reached the front porch yet. How could he possibly be put off by a house he'd never set foot in?

Whatever the reason for his apprehension, he wasn't

leaving. He'd come here looking for Roland Latimer and he wasn't about to give up the search because he'd picked up strange vibes from a house.

Before he could change his mind, Paul hurried up the porch steps and knocked. He'd almost begun to think no one was home when the beveled-glass door finally opened to reveal a tiny gray-haired woman who looked to be around seventy.

She wasn't at all what Paul had expected. His strange aversion to the house had led him to dread an encounter with the occupant. But the twinkle in Zoë Lindstrom's blue eyes reminded him of his grandmother, and he found himself immediately responding to her warm smile.

"You must be the man Audrey sent over," she said as she wiped her hands on her apron.

"I hope my stopping by like this isn't too much of an inconvenience," Paul said apologetically. "Audrey seemed to think it would be okay."

"It's no inconvenience at all. I'm used to people dropping by. Won't you come in?"

It seemed a little odd to Paul that she would be so open and welcoming of a complete stranger in this day and age. He hesitated. "This won't take but a minute. We could speak out here if you prefer."

She gave him an impish smile, as if reading his mind. "I'm a very good judge of character. You don't strike me as the dangerous sort, Mr...."

"Blackstone. Paul Blackstone."

"What a nice, solid name," she said with another smile. "I'm Zoë. Please come in, Mr. Blackstone. Or may I call you Paul?"

"Of course. But before I take up any more of your time, perhaps I should tell you why I'm here."

"Why don't you tell me over tea? I hear the kettle now. Your timing is excellent." She took his arm and pulled him inside. Then, closing the door, she hustled off down a narrow hallway, presumably toward the kitchen. "Please make yourself at home," she called over her shoulder. "The parlor is just to your right."

Paul stood in the foyer for a moment and glanced around. The interior of the house was bright and pleasant, with lots of windows and gleaming hardwood floors. The faint scent of lemon furniture polish lingered in the air, and as he walked into the living area, the old-fashioned, afghan-draped furniture reminded him yet again of his grandmother. A fire crackled behind a metal screen, and the disquiet he'd experienced outside seemed even more incongruous in the midst of such cheerful homeyness.

A few minutes later Zoë returned with a tea tray. She'd removed her apron, and Paul saw that she was dressed in dark slacks and a pale blue sweater that complemented her gray hair and deepened the sapphire of her eyes. She'd undoubtedly been very pretty in her day, but rather than trying to preserve the vestiges of youth, she seemed to have embraced her golden years.

"Here, let me help you with that." Paul took the tray, and she motioned to the table in front of the sofa.

"Just put it there. Thank you so much for your help. Such nice manners," she commented appreciatively. "An attractive but rare quality in young men these days."

Paul didn't feel all that young, but he supposed age, like so many other things, was relative.

Zoë patted the seat beside her. "Please join me. There's nothing like a cup of tea on a chilly day like this. Of course—" She paused as she poured out the tea "—you Seattleites prefer your coffee, don't you?"

"How do you know I'm from Seattle?" Paul asked, surprised yet again by the observation. But then, he supposed his tailored slacks and cashmere sweater was something of a uniform for the thirty-something, urban-dwelling professionals so prevalent in the Emerald City.

Zoë shrugged, giving him the same answer as the young waitress had. "I know you're not from around here."

"No, I'm not. Which is why I came to see you," Paul said as he accepted the delicate demitasse cup. "I'm trying to find someone—a local. Audrey Sylvester told me that you'd lived here longer than she has and might be able to help me."

Zoë picked up her own cup. "Does this person you're looking for have a name?"

"Roland Latimer."

She'd been lifting the teacup to her lips, but now her hand froze in midair as her eyes widened in shock. "*Roland Latimer.* Are you sure that's his name?"

Paul's earlier uneasiness returned as he observed her

reaction. "Positive. My wife met him at a party at the hotel last night."

"But…you didn't meet him yourself?" she asked carefully.

Paul frowned. "No. Why?"

Zoë's hand was steady as she lifted the cup to her lips. Her expression turned pensive. "Did your wife describe him to you?"

"No, she didn't. Look," Paul said impatiently, "do you know this guy or don't you?"

"I'm familiar with the name, but I've never met him. I can assure you, I would have remembered *that*." Zoë gave a wry chuckle as she took another sip of her tea.

"Why do I get the feeling I'm the butt of some inside joke here?" Paul muttered in frustration.

Her blue eyes twinkled over the rim of her cup. "I suppose that's because you are, in a way."

"Meaning?"

She placed her cup and saucer on the table, then returned her attention to Paul. Her eyes were still twinkling, but unless he imagined it, he glimpsed a shadow behind the amusement. "Roland Latimer has been dead for over seventy years. He was killed in the fire that destroyed the original Fernhaven Hotel."

The hair at the back of Paul's neck lifted at her words. "Are you telling me that my wife saw a ghost?" he asked in astonishment.

She laughed again, the sound as light and airy as a wind chime. "Let's hope not! Roland Latimer was a very nasty customer. Alive or dead, I wouldn't want to cross paths with him."

Paul set aside his own tea. "Then I don't understand. Why would Audrey Sylvester lead me to believe that you could help me find him?"

"She meant well, I'm sure. Around here I'm considered something of an expert on local history. I was born on the night of the fire, you see, and I've always had a fascination for the tragedy. I even wrote a book about it years ago. The manuscript was published by a small local press, and only a handful of people outside my own family bought it. But Audrey has always been one of my most devoted fans." Zoë's self-deprecating smile was still charming, even though her words were hardly what Paul had expected. "I suspect that's why she sent you to me. She probably recognized Latimer's name from my book."

That might also explain the younger waitress's startled reaction, Paul thought. But it did nothing to clarify how his wife had conversed with a man who had supposedly been dead for seventy years.

Zoë got up and walked over to one of the built-in bookcases flanking the fireplace. Carefully selecting a volume, she brought it back over to the sofa, then leafed through the pages until she found the one she wanted. "That's Roland Latimer."

She pointed to a photograph of a dark-haired man of about forty. He might have been described by some as handsome, but Paul thought the cruelty in his face gave him a sinister, almost serpentine appearance.

"Who was he?" he asked uneasily.

"A very complicated man, from everything I've been able to learn about him. Complicated…and evil." Zoë shivered as she studied Latimer's photograph. "None of that matters now, though, because I seriously doubt that Latimer is the man your wife saw at the party last night."

She *doubted* it? How could there be any question when Latimer had been dead for decades?

Zoë gave him a regretful smile. "I'm afraid your wife may have been the victim of a practical joke. A couple of the locals have had a bit of fun trying to convince some of the hotel employees that the place is haunted and they've used information from my book to make their stories sound authentic. If the man bothers your wife again, you should call the police. They'll take care of him."

"That's good advice." Almost against his will, Paul glanced at the picture of Latimer. He didn't like looking at the man, but there was something disturbingly familiar about his features. "I appreciate your taking the time to talk to me."

"It was my pleasure." When Paul started to stand, she put her hand on his arm. "Wait—" She jerked her hand back as if she'd been burned. The book slid to the floor with a bang as the color drained from her face.

Paul sat back down. "Are you all right?" he asked in concern. "Do you feel ill?"

"No, it's just…I didn't expect…" Zoë searched his face. "Is there another reason you came to see me, Mr. Blackstone?"

On some level he registered the fact that she had decided not to call him Paul after all. "No, why?"

Her hand had been steady before, but now he noticed a pronounced tremble as she picked up the book and set it on the table. "There isn't something more you want to ask me?"

Paul shrugged. "No, that was it, and I'm sorry I've taken up so much of your time. I really should go."

Her hand clutched his arm and she flinched again. But this time she didn't let go. After a moment her eyes fluttered closed. "Your son," she said softly. "How did he die?"

The blood in Paul's veins turned to ice as he jerked his arm free of her grasp. "How do you know about my son?"

"You're still grieving," she said. "I can see it in your eyes. The loss of a child brings on a special kind of pain."

"How do you know I had a son?" Paul demanded.

"I can...sense these things. I have what some people call 'the gift.'"

"You're psychic?" His voice hardened almost imperceptibly.

"I can't predict the future. But I do have certain abilities. Do you know what a medium is?"

"You communicate with the dead," Paul said.

She nodded solemnly. "Occasionally."

His tone turned contemptuous. "I'm sorry, but I don't believe in any of that stuff."

She smiled. "No need to apologize. Your skepticism doesn't offend me. I've lived with it all my life. I didn't ask for this ability." She clasped her hands in her lap. "There was a time when I would have gladly given it away, but now I just accept it. And if I can help someone along the way—someone like you—so much the better."

"How do you think you can help me?" Paul asked doubtfully.

"Your son was with his mother when he died. She almost crossed over with him, didn't she? That created a powerful bond between them."

Paul's heart began to hammer as he got to his feet. "Who the hell are you? How did you find out those things about my family? Who have you talked to?"

"I'm afraid you wouldn't believe me even if I told you," she murmured.

Anger and disgust washed over him as he stared down at her, challenging her. "You don't have to say another word. I'm familiar with what you do. You prey on grief," he said coldly. "Do you think we haven't been approached by vultures like you before?"

She looked at him, aghast. "I'm afraid you've somehow gotten the wrong impression—"

"I doubt that." He took a moment to get his anger under control. "What I don't know is how you found out about my son. You must have somehow gotten your hands on a guest list and researched everyone who would be at Fernhaven this weekend until you hit upon a likely pigeon. You and Audrey Sylvester must be in this together somehow. I'll just bet she's your most devoted fan." The assistant manager at the hotel had to be in on it, too, Paul realized, since she'd sent him to Audrey Sylvester. That fit. They would need someone on the inside to provide them with a guest list. That also explained why Zoë had so enthusiastically welcomed a complete stranger into her home. No wonder she hadn't been apprehensive. She already knew who he was.

Normally Paul wasn't the conspiracy-theory type, but something was definitely going on here. He was being played for a sucker by these people and he didn't like it one damn bit. And worse, they were attempting to run their scam on Elizabeth.

Paul could see right through them, but Elizabeth… she'd been susceptible to this type of con before. She'd wanted to believe so badly that she could somehow connect with Damon that she'd allowed herself to be taken in by a woman who claimed, just like Zoë Lindstrom, that she had the ability to communicate with the dead.

Elizabeth's therapy had been set back weeks, maybe months, by the unscrupulous "medium," and Paul wasn't about to let that happen again. Elizabeth was stronger now. He could see that with his own eyes. But she was still vulnerable when it came to their son. They both were.

"What you're trying to do is despicable," Paul said with all the loathing he could muster. "If you or anyone else tries to contact my wife again, I'll make you very, very sorry."

Zoë lifted her palms in supplication. "But you came to *me,* Mr. Blackstone. I didn't seek you out. All I want is to help you."

"I'll bet."

She stood and took a step toward him. She was a tiny woman, but it was all Paul could do not to back away from her.

Her eyes…there was something strange about her eyes, he realized. She was looking right at him, but she wasn't *focused* on him. It was as if she was seeing someone else. Or listening to someone else.

"I have a message from your son, Mr. Blackstone."

Icy fingers traced up and down Paul's spine. "Don't," he warned angrily. "Don't use my son's memory in your filthy business."

A terrible sadness seemed to come over the woman then, and she suddenly looked much older than he'd originally thought. "All I want to do is help you."

"You've already helped me by suggesting I go to the police. Under the circumstances, that seems a very good idea."

"But that was before I *knew,*" she persisted. "The police can't help you."

"But you can, right? For a price? Or maybe you call it a donation."

"I don't want your money." She put out a hand to touch him again, but Paul moved away from her. "Just listen to me, please," she begged. "Your son is afraid for his mother." She stopped as if listening for a moment, then said in a strange, whispery voice, "You promised, remember? You promised to watch out for her."

Outrage and shock stormed through Paul as he turned

and strode into the foyer. Flinging open the door, he rushed through, then took the porch steps two at a time, unable to get away from Zoë Lindstrom fast enough.

Behind him he heard her call out to him, but he didn't turn. He didn't slow down until he was all the way back to his car. Sliding behind the wheel, he started the engine, and the tires screamed as he shot away from the curb. But his hands were shaking so badly he was afraid to drive. Just before he reached the bridge, he pulled to the side of the road and parked.

Mist swirled over the hood of his car as he slumped in the seat and scrubbed his face with his hands. Anger drained out of him, leaving behind the grief he'd lived with for so long.

Zoë Lindstrom's cruel game had unleashed a torrent of raw memories. If he closed his eyes, he could still see Damon's face. In his mind he could still hear his son's laughter, feel those sturdy little arms around his neck as if it had only been yesterday that he'd last held him.

Suddenly Paul remembered his son exactly the way he'd been the night before he'd left to go camping with the Braidens. Damon had been so excited about the trip, it was all he'd been able to talk about for weeks. But when Paul had gone into his room to help him pack that night, he'd sensed that his son was troubled about something.

"Damon." Paul sat on the bed and drew the boy down beside him. "Is something wrong, son?"

Damon shook his dark head, refusing to look up.

"Are you sure? Because if something's bothering

*you, you can tell me, you know." When he still didn't an-
swer, Paul said softly, "It's okay if you've changed your
mind about the camping trip. You don't have to go."*

*Damon looked up, his expression stricken. "But I
want to go, Dad. I haven't changed my mind. It's just…"*

"Just what, son?"

"I'm worried about Mom."

*"Why are you worried about your mother?" Paul
asked in surprise. "She'll be fine. You've been away
from her before. Remember that fishing trip you and I
took last year? We were gone almost a week, and she
was perfectly fine when we got back."*

"She missed us, though, didn't she?"

*The look on his son's face almost broke Paul's heart.
"Of course she missed us. We missed her, too. That's
what happens when you go away. You miss the people
you leave behind. But then you start to have so much
fun, you don't even think about home anymore." He
squeezed Damon's shoulders. "You'll probably even be
a little sad when it's time to come back."*

Damon nodded, but he still didn't look convinced.

*"And as for your mother…she and I have plans, too.
We're going away for the weekend. But you can call us
anytime you want. Day or night."*

*Damon glanced up. "You'll watch out for her, won't
you, Dad?"*

"Of course, I will."

"Promise?"

"I promise," Paul said as he pulled his son close.

Damon slipped his arms around Paul's neck and hugged him for a long, long time.

As the memory slipped away, Paul stared out at the mist. He'd thought about that night a lot since Damon's death. The promise his son had asked of him, the way he had hugged Paul so fiercely…it was almost as if he'd somehow known that it would be one of their last times together.

But he couldn't have known. The accident had happened out of the blue. It was one of those tragic, meaningless happenstances that no one could have predicted, least of all a seven-year-old boy who'd had his whole future ahead of him that morning.

Sometimes at night when Paul lay awake, he imagined that Damon was still close by, just down the hall from him. Sometimes, like now, with the memories so vivid, he could almost sense his son's presence. He could almost pretend that Damon was seated beside him and they were off on one of their adventures together. For a moment he even thought he heard his son's voice.

Love you, Dad!

"I love you, too," Paul whispered into the silence.

Chapter Eight

Elizabeth's bedroom door was closed when Paul got back, and he thought she might be taking a nap. He hated to disturb her, but something—his promise to Damon perhaps—compelled him to make sure that she was okay.

He walked over and knocked softly. She didn't respond at first, but then he heard her moving about and knew that she was up. A moment later she drew back the door as she belted a robe around her waist. She'd tied her hair back, but a few damp tendrils curled about her nape. Paul wondered if he'd gotten her out of the tub.

"Sorry to disturb you, but I wanted to let you know that I'm back." His gaze swept over her flushed skin. He could smell the perfume of her bath and he suddenly wanted more than anything to lean down and press his lips to her warm neck.

Then he saw her eyes. They were cold and remote, and his heart sank. He'd been optimistic earlier that he'd been making progress in tearing down the wall between them. He could have sworn last night in her bedroom and this morning at the waterfall that the bond between them had begun to strengthen. But now she seemed more withdrawn than ever. What had happened while he'd been gone?

Refusing to meet his gaze, she came out of her bedroom and closed the door. "It's cold in here." She shivered as she wrapped her arms around her waist.

"I'll light a fire," he offered.

"No, don't bother. We're going out in a little while."

He'd forgotten about the dance later that night in the Glacier Ballroom. The black-tie event was to be a practice run for the staff in order to prepare for the more elaborate affair that had been planned for the hotel's grand opening.

"We don't have to go," he said with a shrug. "We could order in. Have dinner by the fire." He knelt and busied himself with the kindling.

"But that's the whole point of this trip, isn't it? To convince Boyd Carter that you and I are a happily married couple so he'll agree to do business with you?"

Paul couldn't believe she'd just said that. He'd already admitted that his real reason for bringing her up here was to work on their relationship.

Had she forgotten that conversation already? Or was she simply trying to pretend it had never happened?

Once he had the fire going, Elizabeth came over and warmed her hands over the blaze. Paul straightened slowly as he studied her profile. She still wouldn't look at him.

"Is something wrong?" he finally asked.

Her attention remained on the fire. "Where were you this afternoon?"

"I had a meeting with Boyd Carter. I told you that."

"He called two hours ago to let you know that you'd left some papers in his suite. Where did you go after the meeting? You obviously didn't come back here."

Paul hesitated. He didn't really want to tell her that he'd been out looking for Roland Latimer after she'd asked him not to. He decided on a half-truth instead. "I took a drive."

"Alone?"

Paul scowled. "Yes, alone. Why? Did something happen while I was gone?"

"I hiked back up to the waterfall."

His frown deepened. "I don't know if that's such a good idea. It's dangerous up there. You shouldn't go up there alone."

"I wasn't alone."

Paul's heart skipped a beat at her tone. "What do you mean? Someone went with you? Frankie?"

"No, not Frankie. Nina Wilson."

Paul was shocked into silence for a moment. "You went up to the waterfall with Nina Wilson? Why, for God's sakes?"

"We didn't go up there together," Elizabeth said in a strange voice. "I...think she followed me."

Paul swore as he ran a hand through his hair in agitation. "She shouldn't even still be here. I thought she would have checked out hours ago."

"I don't think she's going back to Seattle," Elizabeth said cryptically.

"She said that?"

"She said a lot of things." Elizabeth finally turned to face him, and Paul caught his breath. The dancing flames reflecting in her eyes almost made them appear to glow. She suddenly looked very mysterious. Otherworldly.

Apprehension gripped him. She seemed so…different. He couldn't explain it, but the change that had come over her since he'd left a few hours ago deepened his unease. "What else did she say?"

Elizabeth turned back to the fire. "She admitted that she's in love with you. She said that you love her, too."

The way she said it—almost matter-of-factly—worried Paul more than anything. It was as if she didn't care anymore. "You have to know how ridiculous that is. You heard what I told her last night."

Elizabeth barely lifted one shoulder. "I only heard your end of the conversation. I can't know for sure you were talking to Nina."

"For God's sake, are we back to *that?*" he exploded in frustration. "I'm not in love with Nina Wilson! I don't feel anything for her except disgust. Right now I'm furious enough to wring her neck for what she's trying to pull."

Elizabeth winced at his sudden anger. It was a relief to see a crack in her cold, indifferent facade. "She said you'd say and do anything to keep me appeased until after the divorce."

Paul had been about to deny the charges once again,

but he stopped suddenly. "Wait a minute. How does she know about the divorce?"

Elizabeth's expression turned accusing. "That's what I'd like to know. She seemed to know a lot of things about our marriage. Intimate things."

"She didn't learn them from me. Elizabeth…" Paul tried to take her arm, but she pulled away from him. "I'm telling you the truth. There is nothing going on between Nina and me. I don't know what kind of sick game she's trying to play here, but I promise you one thing—I'm going to find out."

He grabbed his jacket and strode to the door.

Behind him Elizabeth called anxiously, "Where are you going?"

"To have it out with her once and for all."

"Paul, don't."

He glanced over his shoulder. "Don't what?" he demanded angrily. "Don't make waves? Don't prove to you that I'm not an adulterer? Don't make you have second thoughts about this divorce?"

Her eyes widened in surprise.

He gave her a grim little smile. "That's right. I know exactly what you're trying to do. But I'm not going to make it easy for you, Elizabeth."

AFTER THE DOOR SLAMMED behind him, Elizabeth remained frozen at the fireplace, her heart pounding in agitation and her head throbbing from pent-up tension. She lifted a hand to massage the pain at her temples.

Paul was right, of course. Ever since they'd arrived at Fernhaven she'd looked for any excuse not to get close to him because she'd convinced herself that divorce was the right answer.

But she was finding that it wasn't so easy to let go of everything they'd once had together. Paul had been her first love, the father of her child. A part of her would always love him. But being with him...

She drew a deep breath as she gazed into the flames. Being with Paul was just too painful. The memories of what they'd had and what they'd lost were still too raw. There were times when Elizabeth could hardly bear to look at him.

What she felt was not that unusual, Dr. Summers had assured her. The death of a child was a terrible stressor for even the strongest of marriages. Grief and sorrow could either strengthen a couple or tear them apart because each person had his or her own way of coping. And those methods weren't always compatible. Sometimes it was hard to understand or appreciate what the other was going through.

When Paul had gone back to work within a week of the tragedy, Elizabeth had become convinced that he couldn't possibly have loved Damon as much as she. How could he even think about rejoining the land of the living when their only son was dead?

And when he'd eventually suggested that she might want to think about going back to the shop or at least to start sketching again, she'd resented him for trying to instill a sense of normalcy to their lives when nothing was ever going to be normal again.

In time, she'd come to realize that Paul's throwing himself into his work was his own way of coping with grief, just as withdrawing from the world was hers. That the two didn't mesh put an even greater strain on their relationship. They'd eventually drifted so far apart that it seemed pointless to even try and bridge the gulf.

Pointless…and much too painful. Because in order to repair their marriage, they would have to find a way to let go of the past, and Elizabeth didn't think she was ready to do that yet. She might never be.

As the fire died down, the room grew chilly. Rather than throwing on another log, she hurried to the bedroom to dress. But when she opened the door, she stopped on the threshold with a gasp, her gaze frozen on the French doors across the room.

Roland Latimer stood just outside, gazing in at her.

Or…had she only imagined him?

Because suddenly there was nothing outside her door but a thick, rolling mist.

PAUL USED HIS CELL PHONE to call the front desk and asked to be connected to Nina Wilson's room. She took so long to answer that he'd begun to hope that she might have already left for Seattle. When she finally picked up, she sounded out of breath, as if she'd had to hurry to the phone.

"Hello?"

"It's Paul Blackstone. I need to talk to you."

"Paul." Her voice lowered conspiratorially, as if someone might be in the room with her. "I was hoping you'd call. Are you coming up?"

As anxious as he was to have it out with her, Paul knew better than to confront the woman alone in her hotel room. She was either delusional or a very clever troublemaker, and at this point he had no idea what she might be up to. "I'm in the lobby," he said coldly. "You come down."

"I can't. I'm not dressed. I just got out of the shower." She hesitated. "It would be much better if you came up here. You don't have to be afraid," she added playfully. "I won't bite. Unless you want me to, of course."

He gritted his teeth at her suggestive innuendo. "Just throw on some clothes and get down here. This can't wait."

"Oh, all right," she said impatiently. "I'll be down in five minutes."

She took closer to twenty, and when Paul finally spotted her getting off the elevator, he almost didn't recognize her. She looked nothing like the young, professional woman who'd been showing up at his office for the past six months. She'd shed the slender skirts and silk blouses for a pair of tight low-rider jeans and a snug belly-baring sweater.

Walking away from the elevator, she turned to scour the lobby, and for a moment she had her back to Paul. His gaze lit on a tattoo that peeked over the low waist of her jeans, and for some reason that, even more than her suggestive attire, seemed to crystallize for him just how little he knew about the woman.

She'd been a competent, intelligent assistant, but now he had to wonder what had brought her to the attention of his firm's human-resources department in the first place. Fate? Coincidence?

Or something more sinister?

He was probably making too much of this, Paul told himself as he approached her. Since when did he see a conspiracy in everyone's motives?

He called out her name and she turned with a seductive smile. "Paul! I'm so glad you called—"

Taking her arm, he guided her away from the crowd milling about in the lobby to a quiet alcove where he could speak his mind freely without worrying about creating a scene. Not that he much cared at the moment who heard him.

"What the hell are you still doing here?" he asked when they were both seated at a discreet table. "I told you last night to pack up your things and drive back to Seattle."

She tossed her red hair over one shoulder and gave him another smile. "Don't I even get a drink first?"

"This isn't a social visit, Nina. What are you up to?"

Her brows lifted. "I don't know what you mean. I thought you'd be happy that I took the initiative of showing up here last night with those papers you needed. I thought I was being a good assistant."

"And the conversation you had with my wife this afternoon? What was that all about?" Paul demanded.

She frowned. "I don't know what you're talking about."

"You saw Elizabeth at the waterfall this afternoon. You told her that you're in love with me and you implied…that I have feelings for you. Why would you tell her something like that when I've never given you any reason to believe it?"

She looked as if she might try to bluff her way out of the situation, but then she shrugged. "Okay, I did see Elizabeth this afternoon. I did tell her all those things. But it was for her own good. You must see that." She reached over and tried to put her hand on Paul's. When he jerked away, her gaze darkened. "Why are you acting this way? Why are you still trying to deny what we feel for each other?"

"What we *feel* for each other?" His tone implied that she'd gone stark raving mad. Paul wasn't so sure that he was that far off the mark. "You're my assistant. There's never been anything more between us than that."

She gave him a reproachful look. "We both know that's not true. You're lying to Elizabeth and you're lying to yourself. I've seen the way you look at me." She leaned forward, something dark glittering in her eyes. "I know you want me. As much as I want you."

Paul stared at her in cold shock. He couldn't believe this was the same woman with whom he'd worked day in and day out for months. Why had he never picked up on her infatuation before? "You need to listen to me, Nina. Listen to me very carefully. There's nothing between us. There never has been and there never will be. I want you to go back to Seattle and clean out your desk. I don't want to see you when I get back."

Her eyes flooded with sudden tears. She put trembling fingers to her lips. "You don't mean that. You're only saying it because of the divorce."

"How do you even know about the divorce? Someone else must have told you, because I sure as hell didn't."

She sniffed. "It wasn't so difficult to figure out. Your relationship with Elizabeth is hardly a secret. Everyone in the firm knows that you've been estranged ever since Damon—"

Paul reached out and grabbed her arm. "Don't you dare bring my son into this."

She pulled away from him and massaged her arm where he'd clutched her. "I'm sorry. I've handled this whole thing badly, haven't I?" Her eyes were dry now and gleaming with something Paul couldn't define. She seemed capable of turning her emotions on and off at the blink of an eye. "I understand where you're coming from. A man in your position can't be too careful. If Elizabeth were to try to use our relationship as leverage in the settlement—"

"There is no relationship," Paul said hotly. "Get that through your head. I don't know whether you're delusional or some kind of operator, but whatever your motive, it won't work on me. I'm in love with my wife."

When Nina lifted her gaze, he saw that her eyes had

gone cold. Cold…and dangerous. "I'm not the one who's trying to fool you, Paul. Elizabeth isn't the person you think she is. She's not just troubled. She's seriously demented. She even tried to kill me this afternoon. Did she tell you that?" Nina searched his face for a moment, then smiled grimly. "No, I thought not."

"What are you talking about?" he asked incredulously.

"It happened when we were up at the waterfall this afternoon." Nina bit her lip. "Elizabeth tried to push me off the cliff."

"You're lying."

Her eyes widened in distress. "I'm not! She pushed me. I felt her hand on my back. We were the only two there, so it had to be her. I don't want to go to the police, for your sake, but if you refuse to believe me, what choice do I have?"

Paul leaned across the table and lowered his voice. "If you want to call the police, go ahead. I have a few things I'd like to say to them, as well. You do whatever you have to do, but you stay the hell away from my wife. If you go near her again—"

"You'll what?" Nina's green eyes flamed with sudden anger. "Are you *threatening* me?"

"I'm warning you," Paul said. "You have no idea who you're dealing with. I'll do whatever is necessary to protect my family."

She gave him a pitying look then. "What family? Your son is dead and your wife is just an empty shell. They're gone, Paul. There's no one left to protect."

ELIZABETH WAS SEATED on the sofa in the living room when he returned. She jumped to her feet the moment he walked through the door, and Paul noticed immediately how pale and edgy she seemed.

This thing with Nina Wilson was really getting to her. He wanted to take her reaction as a sign that she still cared, but somehow he didn't think any good could come from the situation. He had no idea what Nina was up to, but he had a feeling she was going to cause a great deal of trouble before she went away.

"What happened?" Elizabeth asked anxiously. "Did you talk to her?"

"Yeah, we talked." Paul walked over to the bar to pour himself a drink.

"What did she say?"

Was it his imagination, or did Elizabeth seem overly agitated? She followed him to the bar and stood tugging at the tiny diamond moon she wore around her neck. She only grew fidgety like that when she was overwrought about something.

Was she worried about what he'd found out?

The moment the notion occurred to Paul, Nina's accusation came rushing back.

She's not just troubled. She's seriously demented. She even tried to kill me this afternoon. Did she tell you that?

Paul swallowed the whiskey and poured himself another.

Elizabeth touched his arm. "What did she say?"

He couldn't quite look at her for some reason. "She admitted what she said to you at the waterfall."

"That she's in love with you? And that you feel the same way about her?"

Paul turned. "Yes. She admitted everything." He paused. "She also said that you tried to kill her."

Elizabeth gasped. "You didn't believe her."

"Of course not."

"It was an accident," she whispered.

A fist of fear closed around Paul's heart. "Then something did happen."

Elizabeth nodded. "She slipped on the wet moss, just the way I did earlier. I grabbed her and pulled her back from the edge, but she claimed I pushed her. I swear I never touched her until I grabbed her arm to keep her from falling." She stared at him beseechingly. "You believe me, don't you?"

"Yes, of course I do." He knocked back his second drink and poured a third.

"What is she going to do?" Elizabeth asked worriedly. "You don't think she'd actually go to the police, do you—"

"She won't go to the police. I'll make sure of that."

Their gazes collided in the mirror over the bar. Elizabeth moistened her lips. "What do you mean?"

Paul set aside his drink and turned to place his hands on her arms. "Let me handle this, okay? I don't want you worrying about Nina Wilson. I'll take care of her."

"But Paul—"

"Let's just forget about her for tonight." He dropped his hands from her arms. "Are you sure you want to go to this thing later?"

The abrupt subject change seemed to catch Elizabeth by surprise. Then she glanced across the room at her closed bedroom door and shuddered. "I think it would be good for both of us to get out of here for a while, don't you?"

"If that's what you want." She obviously didn't relish spending the evening alone with him, but at least they were communicating. Her eyes, though, were still cool and remote, her tone that of a polite stranger. They had history, yes, and there had once been so much love between them. But that had been a long time ago.

Paul was suddenly filled with despair. No matter what happened in the next few days, he knew he had to somehow accept the fact that the woman he'd fallen in love with thirteen years ago was never coming back to him.

WHEN HE CAME OUT OF his bedroom a little while later, Elizabeth was already dressed and waiting for him in the living room. She stood at the fireplace, seemingly absorbed by the blaze, and didn't look up as he stepped into the room.

Paul remained motionless, watching her. He couldn't help himself. He'd always thought her a beautiful woman, but since they'd arrived at Fernhaven he'd noticed a change in her. She seemed to glow with an ethereal quality he didn't understand. It was almost as if she no longer belonged to this world—to *his* world—and the notion left him cold and scared.

Tonight she wore a gown of gleaming black satin that clung subtly to her soft curves. The neckline—what he could see of it—was demure enough, but when she turned slightly away from him, he saw that the back plunged below her waistline. Her only jewelry was the crescent moon, which she'd suspended from a long chain and turned so that it cascaded down her back, allowing the diamonds to glitter against her bare skin. Paul had never seen anything so provocative in his life.

His heart pounded in awareness as he cleared his throat to draw her attention. She whirled, and for a moment she, too, appeared breathless. Then she smiled almost shyly. "You always could wear a tux."

She walked toward him, and with every step Paul's heart beat harder. When she reached up to straighten his bow tie, it was all he could do not to catch her hand and lift it to his lips.

Their eyes met and she smiled again. "You look nice tonight."

"So do you." He paused. "More than nice." He couldn't help himself. He caught her hand. "Elizabeth—"

She waited expectantly.

"You look—" He was suddenly at a loss. To tell her that she was the most beautiful woman in the world to him would have seemed too much of a cliché. But she was and always had been. She grew lovelier with each passing year, and he couldn't imagine what his life would be like without her.

"Is something wrong?" she finally asked.

"No. I'm just happy that you came up here with me," he said gruffly. He squeezed her hand. "In spite of everything, I'm glad we've had this time together."

The wistfulness in her eyes tore at Paul's heart. "I'm glad I came, too. But please don't expect it to change anything. Not overnight. So much has happened between us. I don't think we can ever get back what we lost. Maybe it's too late to even try."

"Don't say that. It's not too late." It couldn't be too late. He wouldn't let it be. He lifted her hand to his lips. "Maybe what we should do is concentrate on the moment and stop worrying so much about the future."

Elizabeth closed her eyes on a shudder and pulled her hand away. "I don't know if I can do that. I don't want to fool you into thinking things are going to be different when we leave here. I'm not the same person I was eighteen months ago. I'm not the woman you fell in love with."

Paul swallowed past the lump in his throat. "I'm beginning to realize that."

"Then maybe it would be best to let me go."

"Not without a fight." He tugged her to him.

"Paul—" She placed her hands flat against his chest, a token resistance which he ignored.

"Stop fighting it," he said fiercely. "Just close your eyes and let it happen."

Something sparked in her eyes—passion or anger, he

wasn't sure which. Then her lids fluttered closed as she lifted her lips to his.

Her body trembled against his as he slid his arms around her waist and held her close. She moaned into his mouth, then drew back abruptly, as if the sound startled her. Their gazes met briefly and then, placing her hands on either side of his face, she pulled him to her for another kiss, this one even more passionate and desperate than the first.

Time stood still for Paul. Nothing in the world mattered but the feel of Elizabeth in his arms, the sweep of her tongue against his, the pounding of her heartbeat against his. He wished the moment could last forever…or lead to the inevitable.

But all too soon Elizabeth was pulling away from him, her expression resigned as she stared up at him.

She touched a fingertip to her lips. "That shouldn't have happened."

"Why not? We're still married. And whether you're ready to admit it or not, we still love each other. Why shouldn't we express it?"

"Because it only confuses the issue," she said.

"Don't you mean it confuses you? I'm not the least bit confused," Paul said. "I know exactly what I want."

"But you're putting too much pressure on us! We can't fix our marriage in one short weekend. It's too much to ask."

"We can start," he insisted. "Just give it a chance. Give *us* a chance."

She glanced down. "I don't know if I can. I'm scared."

"I'm scared, too," he said softly. "I'm scared of losing someone else I love." He tilted her head so that he could look into her eyes. "I know exactly how you feel, Elizabeth. I'm right there with you, remember? I know that every time you look at me, you see Damon. I see him in you, too. The way you smile. The way you say certain words." He drew a ragged breath. "There were times when I could hardly stand to look at you because you were so much like him. And, yes, there were times when I thought it would be easier if we just went our separate ways. At least then we wouldn't be constantly reminded of what we'd lost. But it wouldn't help. It wouldn't make losing our son any easier, and I don't think I could bear losing you, too."

A tear spilled over and ran down her cheek. She didn't say a word, but when she took a tentative step toward him, Paul wrapped his arms around her and held her for a very long time.

Chapter Nine

The festivities were well under way by the time Elizabeth and Paul arrived at the Glacier Ballroom later that night. As they entered through the double doors, Elizabeth had the strangest sensation of having stepped back in time. The room was magnificent with its hand-painted frescoes and elaborate domed ceiling, which was an exact replica of the original. High arched windows looked out on a manicured garden draped with tiny fairy lights that twinkled like stars against a backdrop of night and shadow.

From a dais at one end of the ballroom the orchestra played something old-fashioned and romantic as couples glided across the polished marble floor, the women's swirling gowns a kaleidoscope of silks and satins that shimmered sumptuously beneath the imported chandeliers. A champagne fountain flowed freely near buffet tables laden with delicacies and adorned with ice sculptures and crystal bowls of floating orchids. In every corner banks of flowers—cyclamens, camellias and stargazer lilies—were showcased brilliantly against a background of feathery ferns and stately palm trees.

No expense had been spared even for a trial run, and Elizabeth could only imagine what the owners of the hotel had planned for the actual grand opening.

Her arm was looped through Paul's as they stood just inside the doorway. She wasn't quite certain how that had happened. Earlier he'd had someone from the hotel pick them up at the cottage so that she wouldn't have to walk even so short a distance in her high heels. He'd taken her hand to help her out of the golf cart, but afterward Elizabeth couldn't quite remember when or why she'd slipped her arm through his. But here they stood, joined together as if the last eighteen months hadn't ripped them asunder.

As if sensing that she might pull away from him at any moment, Paul placed his hand over hers and squeezed. Elizabeth tilted her head to look at him. Neither of them said anything, but for the longest time their gazes clung.

Elizabeth shivered, not from the cold draft that had followed them inside but from the sudden heat in her husband's eyes. He wanted her. More than ever, he seemed to be telling her.

Drawing a deep, quivering breath, she tore her gaze away just as Frankie came up beside her. She wore one of Elizabeth's designs, too, a metallic satin sheath that draped her lush curves like liquid silver. She'd pulled her dark hair back and rimmed her gray eyes with kohl, giving them an exotic tilt at the corners.

"There you are," she said to Elizabeth. "I wondered if you were going to make it." She glanced past Elizabeth and nodded. "Hello, Paul."

He nodded back. "Frankie."

The greeting was about as cold and perfunctory as Elizabeth could imagine.

"Would you mind if I borrowed Elizabeth for a moment? I need to have a word with her," Frankie said coolly. "It's business. You understand, don't you, Paul?"

Rather than relinquishing his hold on Elizabeth, his grip tightened on her hand. "Can it wait? I've been looking forward all day to dancing with my wife."

Frankie arched a brow as she turned her attention back to Elizabeth. Something that might have been worry—or anger—glinted in her eyes. "This won't take but a minute, Elizabeth. I really do need to talk to you."

"If it's business, perhaps it could wait until we get back to the shop on Tuesday," Elizabeth heard herself murmur.

It obviously wasn't the answer Frankie had wanted or expected. She shrugged, but her expression hardened. "If that's what you want."

"I'll talk to you later, okay?" Elizabeth said over her shoulder as she allowed Paul to lead her onto the dance floor. She didn't like putting Frankie off. They'd been partners and friends for years, and Frankie had always been someone she could count on. But this animosity toward Paul…where had it come from?

She'd have a long talk with Frankie when they got

back on Tuesday, Elizabeth decided. Maybe it was time she and her partner cleared the air about a few things. And maybe while they were at it, they needed to set some boundaries. Elizabeth had always confided freely in her friend, but she wondered now if she'd been a little too open about her personal life.

The moment Paul took her in his arms, however, Elizabeth forgot about Frankie. She forgot about everything except the feel of her husband's hand on her bare back, the brush of his cheek against hers, the whisper of his breath in her ear.

They were waltzing, Elizabeth realized as they swirled and glided over the dance floor. She didn't even know she *could* waltz. But she shouldn't have been surprised that she was able to follow Paul's lead. He'd always been a good dancer. He was good at so many things. An elegant, charming man of many talents, not the least of which was his ability to sweep her off her feet after all these years.

He pulled her even closer, and Elizabeth's heart began to hammer as the tempo increased. The hall had seemed chilly before, but now she grew heated and dizzy as dancers spun in a blur all around them. An awful uneasiness came over her. Something wasn't right about all this. She shouldn't be here. Not with Paul. She wanted to push him away suddenly, but she didn't know why.

And then she saw him.

Roland Latimer stood outside one of the arched windows, his expression dark and angry as he watched Elizabeth and Paul sweep past him.

Elizabeth wanted to say something to Paul, but she couldn't seem to find her voice. Her heart was beating too fast. What if Latimer disappeared, as he had earlier outside her bedroom window? What if he...wasn't real?

As their gazes met over Paul's shoulder, Latimer put out a hand and beckoned to her. When she didn't respond, he pressed his long, pale fingers to the window, and Elizabeth could have sworn she felt his cold touch at the back of her neck.

She stumbled, but Paul caught her easily. "Are you okay?"

She looked past him to the window.

No one was there.

"Elizabeth?"

Her gaze darted back to Paul. "I feel a little light-headed," she murmured. "Maybe I've had enough dancing for one night."

"We'll sit this one out then." Paul took her elbow and led her from the floor. "Would you like something to drink? Some punch or champagne?"

"No champagne." She was already seeing things. She certainly didn't need alcohol to diminish what remained of her faculties.

"Some punch then. I'll be right back."

Elizabeth nodded. She couldn't seem to shake her uneasiness. She didn't know what had happened to her on the dance floor, but she was certain her dizziness had something to do with Roland Latimer. His sudden appearance had scared her even though she wasn't even sure that he was real. And that prospect frightened her even more.

He had to be real, though, because she'd talked to him the evening before. He'd touched her hand.

But how could a flesh-and-blood man just disappear?

It made no sense. Unless, of course, she was going crazy. A conclusion that wasn't as farfetched as Elizabeth would have liked.

While she waited for Paul, she walked over to the window to peer out. She could see nothing on the terrace but mist and shadows.

Lifting her hand, she pressed her fingertips to the window. She expected the glass to be cold to her touch, but instead it was warm, like human flesh.

She started and whirled when someone tapped her shoulder.

"Sorry," Frankie said with a weak smile. "I didn't mean to startle you." She nodded toward the window. "What are you looking at?" she asked curiously.

"I…thought I saw someone out there," Elizabeth murmured.

"Who?"

She hesitated. "Someone I met here last night. The man you saw me talking to on the terrace."

Frankie frowned. "I told you, I didn't see anyone with you last night. I thought you were talking to yourself."

Perhaps she had been, Elizabeth thought uneasily. "What did you want to see me about earlier?"

"You said you wanted to wait until we get back to Seattle," Frankie said a bit peevishly. "I wouldn't want to interrupt your vacation with shop talk."

"This isn't a vacation," Elizabeth hastened to remind her.

Frankie cocked her head. "No? You could have fooled me, the way you and Paul are acting so lovey-dovey all of a sudden. What's going on, Elizabeth? Are you two back together?"

"We're not back together. But things are a bit…confusing," Elizabeth admitted.

Frankie's scowl deepened. "In what way?"

"I don't know. Sometimes I wonder…" Elizabeth trailed off and glanced out the window.

"You wonder what?"

She shrugged. How could she explain her conflicting emotions about Paul when she didn't understand them herself? How could she admit that she suddenly felt she might be losing control again when she'd spent the past few months trying to convince everyone she was well?

"Lizzy, what's wrong?" Frankie asked worriedly.

Elizabeth turned. "Nothing. I'm just a little tired, that's all."

Frankie gave her a reproachful look. "We've been friends and partners for nearly ten years. Sometimes I think I know you better than I know myself. Is Paul pressuring you to reconcile?" When Elizabeth didn't respond, Frankie's eyes glittered angrily. "I thought it had to be something like that. Don't let him do this to you."

"You don't understand—"

Frankie shoved back a stray lock of hair. "Oh, I understand, all right. Paul is a very persuasive man and the two of you have a lot of history. But need I remind you that a week ago you were all set to divorce him as soon as you returned to Seattle? You had reasons for wanting to start a new life, Elizabeth, and those reasons are still valid."

"I know that."

"So you're still going through with the divorce?"

Elizabeth glanced away, suddenly unable to meet Frankie's accusing eyes. Which was ridiculous. Why should she feel guilty about having second thoughts?

"I don't know what I'm going to do," she finally said.

Frankie sighed and folded her arms across her chest. "I was afraid of something like this when you agreed to come up here with him. I should have said something before we left Seattle, but I was hoping..." She paused. "I was hoping it wouldn't come to this."

Elizabeth's pulse quickened at the look on Frankie's face. "Come to what? What are you talking about?"

Frankie glanced around, as if making certain she wouldn't be overheard. "I found out something. I wasn't going to tell you, but under the circumstances, I think you have a right to know." She put her hand on Elizabeth's arm. "It's about Paul."

Elizabeth's heart beat painfully against her chest. "What about him?"

"Evidently he's in some kind of trouble at work."

Elizabeth didn't believe that for a moment. Paul was a brilliant businessman. She couldn't imagine anyone being dissatisfied with his performance. "What kind of trouble?"

Frankie glanced around again before she answered. "I have an acquaintance who works at Paul's firm. She said that he's not exactly on the best of terms with the other partners. A couple of major deals he put together have fallen through in the past year, and he invested a lot of his own money in both projects. When they didn't pan out, he lost a small fortune. I can't help thinking that now would not exactly be the best time for him to have to pony up money in a divorce settlement."

Elizabeth didn't want to listen to Frankie's accusations, but she couldn't bring herself to walk away. She had to hear the rest even if she didn't believe a word of it. "Where did you hear this?"

"I told you, I know someone who works at Paul's firm."

"Who? Give me a name."

"I can't do that. I promised I wouldn't say anything and I don't want to get anyone in trouble for carrying tales away from the office. But what if it's true? Think about it, Lizzy." Frankie bit her lip. "Did Paul show even the slightest bit of interest in rekindling your relationship until you wanted out? He was perfectly happy to go along with the way things were until he figured out how much a divorce would cost him."

"You don't know that," Elizabeth said coldly. "You

don't like him for some reason and so you're willing to think the worst of him."

"That's not true. I never had anything against him until…" Frankie's gaze shifted away from Elizabeth's.

"Until what?" Elizabeth pressed.

"How can you just forget about *her?*"

"You mean Nina Wilson?" Elizabeth hadn't forgotten about Nina Wilson. Not for a moment. "It's not what you think, Frankie."

"How can you be so sure?"

"Because Paul told me there's nothing between them, and I believe him."

"Because you *want* to believe him," Frankie accused. "You've always had a blind spot where he's concerned."

Elizabeth's voice hardened with anger. "He's still my husband. If I choose to believe him, that's my business."

"And I'm supposed to just keep my mouth shut and let you get taken for a ride? I'm sorry, but I can't do that. He's lying to you, Lizzy. Why can't you see that?"

"And why can't you see that this is none of your business?" Elizabeth said bluntly.

Frankie looked crushed by the rebuke. Then she shrugged. "Fine, if that's the way you want it. I'll stay out of it. But answer one question for me. If there's nothing between Paul and Nina Wilson, why is it he can't seem to stay away from her?"

She turned and stalked off, and as Elizabeth watched her disappear into the crowd, she suddenly felt bereft. She was still angry at Frankie for her insinuations and interference, but they'd been close for a long time. She didn't want to lose Frankie's friendship.

How had it come to this? Elizabeth wondered in despair. How had she allowed herself to become so isolated, first from her husband and now from her best friend?

The answer was obvious, of course. Since Damon's death she'd merely been drifting from one day to the next while life had gone on for everyone else. It was as if she'd just awakened from a Rip Van Winkle-type sleep and now she had to face the terrible realization that she no longer knew the people who had once been closest to her.

Elizabeth suddenly felt very lost. She started to go after Frankie, but then she froze as the crowd parted slightly and she caught a glimpse of Nina Wilson.

Even from across the room Elizabeth could see that her red hair was askew and one of the thin straps of her gown had slipped down her arm.

She had the look of a woman freshly returned from a tryst with her lover, and a moment later Paul stepped into the room behind her.

Chapter Ten

Elizabeth stood shivering on the terrace. She hadn't taken the time to grab a wrap, but instead had rushed through the nearest French doors, unable to face the sight of Paul and Nina Wilson together.

She couldn't forget what Frankie had asked her only moments earlier. *If there's nothing between Paul and Nina Wilson, why is it he can't seem to stay away from her?*

Deep down Elizabeth knew that she was jumping to conclusions. After she'd defended her husband so fiercely to Frankie, she should have had the guts to walk across the room and confront him openly with her suspicions.

But she hadn't been able to do it. She hadn't been able to do anything except run away. And that reaction probably spoke more to her emotional state than it did to Paul's fidelity. Her willingness, even for one brief moment, to assume the worst of him should have told her all she needed to know about a possible reconciliation. If she couldn't bring herself to trust him—was unable to take him at his word—what chance did their marriage have?

Besides, it was easier this way, wasn't it? Easier to just keep drifting than to fight her way back to him. To wake up and live again. To love again. To endure pain again.

In some ways, seeing Paul with Nina had almost been a relief.

Restless with her thoughts, Elizabeth walked over to the edge of the terrace and stared into the darkness. Beyond the man-made swimming pool was a series of smaller natural pools fed by the underground hot springs for which the original hotel had been famous. The architect had painstakingly incorporated the pools into the natural landscaping, giving them each a private, woodsy setting.

Elizabeth heard the faint sound of laughter from one of the pools, and she wondered if a couple of the guests had stolen away from the dance to go skinny-dipping by moonlight. She and Paul had done that once in Jamaica. Stripped off all their clothes on a moonlit beach and run laughing into the water. Elizabeth couldn't imagine doing that now. She couldn't imagine feeling that free and unencumbered.

She hadn't realized that she was crying until she felt a tear trickle down her cheek. She lifted a hand to wipe it away.

"Elizabeth…"

Her name was barely a whisper. A trick of the wind, she thought.

But then it came again. More demanding this time.

"Elizabeth…"

The blood in her veins turned to ice. Everything inside her stilled as she slowly turned.

She saw nothing at first. And then, just as he had the night before, he seemed to materialize from the mist.

He stood before her, a dark, commanding figure with no more substance than a shadow.

Elizabeth's heart pounded as he walked toward her. He moved with a peculiar ease and grace that almost made him appear to float. But that was impossible.

Or was it?

Maybe he wasn't real, after all. Maybe her subconscious had conjured him from the mist and shadows, but for what reason, Elizabeth had no idea.

Real or not, she wanted to turn and run from him, but she couldn't move. She stood paralyzed, unable to tear her gaze from his.

It was his eyes, she realized with a punch of panic. They were hypnotic. Mesmerizing. So black and piercing, she had a feeling they could penetrate her very soul.

"Don't be afraid of me," he said in that whispery, dark voice.

She was terrified, but she was also drawn to him in a way she couldn't explain.

Elizabeth closed her eyes. When she opened them, he was still there, and she started to tremble as the dread inside her deepened. "Who are you? Why are you following me?"

He was even larger than she remembered. Daunting and formidable, his aristocratic features might have been chiseled from pale granite. "You've come," he said. "At long last, you've come back to me. I've been waiting so long…."

She put a nervous hand to her throat. "What are you talking about? You don't even know me." Her voice had a strange breathless quality that she hardly recognized as her own.

"That isn't true, Elizabeth. I know everything about you. Your thoughts are my thoughts. Your pain is my own. I know you…because I'm a part of you."

Elizabeth gasped. Everything about him frightened her, and yet she couldn't seem to rip herself free of him.

He moved even closer to her then. When he put up a hand to touch her face, Elizabeth cringed. She wanted to stop him, but she couldn't. It was as if he'd cast a dark spell over her, and yet she couldn't shake the notion that this was somehow inevitable. And a part of her wanted to be here with him.

"Remember me?" His fingers brushed along the side of her face, a cool, slippery touch that made her shiver. "Remember me, Elizabeth?"

And suddenly she did. As the image came rushing back, her eyes widened in recognition. "I've seen you before. At this very place. You were at the ground-breaking ceremony last year. I…caught you staring at me."

His gaze deepened. "I knew from the moment I first saw you that we were meant to be together. You belong here with me. That's why you came back."

The proprietary note in his voice jarred Elizabeth. Who was he? And why, oh, why couldn't she break away from him? She had to be dreaming. "I didn't come here because of you. I came up here with my husband."

"Your husband." He gave a dismissive wave of his elegant hand, as if he were shooing away a pesky fly. "He failed you. He isn't worthy of you."

Elizabeth immediately leaped to Paul's defense, just as she had earlier with Frankie. "You don't know him. You don't know anything about him or me."

The dark eyes burned with anger. "Let him go, Elizabeth. I command it."

"How dare you—"

His long, pale fingers stroked down her face yet again, silencing her. "He can never know you the way I know you. He can't feel your sorrow the way I feel it." His cold touch drew a shiver from deep within her. "He can't give you...what I can give you."

He pulled away from her then as he turned his attention to the misty darkness beyond the terrace. Reluctantly Elizabeth followed his gaze. She searched the shadows, saw nothing at first, and then the fog parted.

A small figured darted into her view, there one moment, gone the next.

"Damon." His name slipped through Elizabeth's cold lips on a whisper. She clutched her hands to her heart. "Damon!" She tried to rush toward the vision, but Roland Latimer was suddenly blocking her way.

Elizabeth had the sense that she could go right through him, but she didn't dare try.

"Get out of my way!" she cried. "I have to go to my son!"

"Not yet," he murmured with a smile. "But soon…"

And then he faded into nothing but mist.

ELIZABETH'S EYES FLEW open as she called out her son's name. "Damon?"

"Take it easy," a soft voice soothed her.

"Oh, God, where is he? Where's my son?"

"Elizabeth, can you hear me?" that same voice asked worriedly. "Do you know who I am?"

A face peered down at her in the darkness, and Elizabeth thought at first it was Roland Latimer. Her heart slammed against her chest as she shrank away from him.

"It's okay. Don't be frightened."

She recognized then the gentle voice and probing blue eyes of her therapist. "Dr. Summers?" Had she been dreaming? Had she been lying on the couch in his office this whole time?

The cold stones beneath her bare back brought her sharply back to reality. She lifted a weak hand to her forehead. "What happened?"

"You fainted," he informed her.

"Fainted?" She tried to sit up, but her head was still spinning. Groaning, she closed her eyes. "I feel sick."

"I'm not surprised. Just lie still. You'll feel better soon."

Drawing in a deep, cold breath, Elizabeth stared up at him. His blond hair gleamed golden in the moonlight. He looked very handsome and sophisticated in his tuxedo, and she thought how strange it was to see him like this. Out of his element, so to speak.

She touched his arm. "Are you real?"

She could tell the question took him by surprise. His laugh seemed a bit strained. "Yes, quite real. Why do you ask?"

I've been seeing things, she wanted to tell him. *A man who can materialize from mist. My dead son…*

She blinked back sudden tears and glanced away. "How did you know where to find me?"

"I saw you earlier inside and you looked upset. When you rushed out here, I decided to follow you and make sure you were okay. Luckily I managed to catch you before you hit the stone floor." He lifted her wrist and timed her pulse. "Still rapid," he murmured. "Perhaps we should get you to a hospital."

"Hospital?" she said in alarm. "I don't think that's necessary. People pass out all the time. It's nothing to worry about, is it?"

"Probably not," he agreed. "But it wouldn't hurt to get you checked out just the same, maybe have some blood work done."

"But I'm feeling better," Elizabeth insisted. "I just got a little overheated from dancing." With an effort she sat up and glanced around. "Was—did you see anyone when you came out here?"

His expression remained neutral, but his eyes searched her face. "Why do you ask?"

Elizabeth shivered. "Passing out is embarrassing enough, but I'd hate to think there were witnesses."

He seemed to relax at her response. "No need to be embarrassed, but if it makes you feel better, you were quite alone on the terrace."

Somehow she'd known he was going to say that. Elizabeth wished his assurance made her feel better, but it didn't. Just the opposite. She really had imagined Roland Latimer. And Damon.

What was happening to her? Why was her mind conjuring these images? What did they mean? That she was losing control again?

"Elizabeth! My God, what happened?" She jumped at the sound of Paul's voice. He'd come through the French doors, and when he spotted her lying on the terrace, he rushed over and knelt beside her. "What happened?" he asked again.

"She fainted," Dr. Summers told him.

The therapist's tone changed when he spoke to Paul. The soothing tone was suddenly edged with disapproval, and Elizabeth wondered why. She had the disturbing notion that the two of them were keeping secrets from her. She hadn't felt so alone in months, and experiencing isolation and alienation from those around her was yet another bad sign.

Paul turned anxious eyes on Elizabeth. "Are you okay?"

"I'm fine." She forced a lightness to her voice she

was far from feeling. "I got a little overheated while we were dancing. It's nothing to worry about."

Paul frowned down at her. "I wish I'd known you were feeling so ill. We could have left earlier."

"I didn't know it myself until I came out for some air. But I'm fine now." When she tried to stand, both men rushed to help her. When she was on her feet, both pairs of male hands reached to steady her.

"You must be freezing." Paul shrugged out of his jacket and wrapped it around her shoulders. "Let's get you back to the cottage."

"She's still a little unsteady on her feet," Dr. Summers said coolly. "Why don't I stay with her while you alert someone from the hotel? I've seen some golf carts around, I think."

"That won't be necessary." Before Elizabeth could object, Paul swept her up into his arms.

"You can't carry me all the way back to the cottage," she protested.

"I can and I will. Besides, it's not that far." Paul's arms tightened around her as if he had no intention of ever letting her go.

It had been a long time since he'd held her that way. Elizabeth had forgotten what it was like to feel so warm and protected in his arms. She wanted to revel in Paul's nearness, but she almost instantly recoiled from her feelings, as if her sudden desire for her husband was somehow forbidden.

She hadn't realized that Dr. Summers had followed

them to the cottage until Paul handed him the key. Once he had the door open for them, Paul carried her straight into the bedroom and put her gently on the bed. He took off her shoes and then drew a blanket around her shoulders.

"You don't have to treat me like an invalid," she said with a frown.

"You fainted," Paul said. "That worries me."

"Well, stop worrying. I'm fine."

Dr. Summers walked around to the other side of the bed and lifted her wrist. "Pulse is almost normal." He pressed the back of his hand to her forehead. "You don't seem to be running a temperature."

"That's because I'm not sick," Elizabeth said impatiently. "And I really don't like all this hovering."

Dr. Summers ignored her complaint. "When was the last time you had something to eat?"

She shrugged. "I don't remember. Breakfast, I guess."

"You didn't have lunch?" Paul asked in surprise.

"I walked back up to the waterfall, remember?"

He didn't look happy to be reminded of that. "We should have ordered dinner before we went out, but I thought we'd get something at the dance."

"I'm a grown woman. If I get hungry, I'm perfectly capable of ordering room service."

"Yes, well, you need to start taking better care of yourself," Dr. Summers advised her. "I think it would be a good idea to make an appointment with your physician for a complete checkup when you get back to Seattle. And I'd like you to come in for a session next week."

"But I don't have an appointment until week after next."

"Call my office. We'll work something out." Glancing across the bed at Paul, he said, "Would you mind if I have a few minutes alone with Elizabeth?"

Paul looked as if he did mind, but he shrugged and nodded. "Sure."

When he stepped out of the room and closed the door, Dr. Summers sat down on the edge of Elizabeth's bed. "Is there something you'd like to talk about?"

"What do you mean?" Her stomach was in knots, and she suddenly wanted more than anything to confide everything she'd been experiencing since arriving at Fernhaven. Her conflicting emotions about Paul. The strange visions. Her self-doubts. She badly needed Dr. Summers' reassurance that she wasn't losing her grip on reality, but she had to watch herself. Confessions could backfire. If she wasn't careful, she could find herself back in the psych ward.

"Earlier you asked about Damon," Dr. Summers said. "When you came to, you called out his name, as if you expected him to be there."

Elizabeth bit her lip. "I wondered when you'd get around to that."

"Do you want to talk about it?" he asked in that mildly interested but nonjudgmental way he had.

"There's really nothing to talk about."

His blue eyes probed her face. "Are you sure?"

"What is it that you want me to say?" she asked in frustration.

"Whatever it is you want to tell me."

The doublespeak could drive a person crazy, Elizabeth thought with no small amount of irony. She turned and watched the mist outside her bedroom window. "Can I ask you a question, for a change?"

"Of course."

"Do you believe in ghosts?"

When he didn't answer immediately, she turned back to him. "Well?"

Still he hesitated. When he finally spoke, Elizabeth had a feeling that he was choosing his words carefully. "I believe in ghosts, but I think they're manifested from the living rather than from the dead."

Elizabeth sighed. "Somehow I knew you'd say that. Ghosts are a product of our own imaginations. A symptom of some deep-rooted worry or fear."

"That's what I believe, yes. But what do you believe, Elizabeth?"

"I'd rather tell you what I know. I know my son is dead. I know he can't come back to me."

"And?"

Her gaze lifted to his. "And if I told you what I saw tonight, you'd think I'm crazy."

"I doubt that." He gave her an encouraging smile. "Why don't you try me?"

She shivered in spite of the blanket Paul had covered her with earlier. "What if I told you I saw a ghost tonight?"

"You mean Damon?"

She drew a painful breath. "A man. A stranger named Roland Latimer who says he knows me. He says he's been waiting for me."

"Waiting for you?" Dr. Summers's expression turned pensive.

Elizabeth nodded. "And the odd thing is, I remember seeing him here last year when Paul and I came up for the ground-breaking ceremony. I saw him staring at me, and it was like…I don't know…he formed some sort of connection with me. I can't explain it, but I think he's been with me ever since I saw him that day."

"You mean he's been following you? Stalking you?" Dr. Summers frowned. "That doesn't sound like a ghost, Elizabeth."

"Yes," she said softly. "It does. Ever since those strange things started happening in Damon's room, I've been researching the supernatural. I even consulted a medium, remember?"

"Yes, I remember. And as I also recall, she turned out to be a con artist with a rap sheet a mile long."

Elizabeth winced. She'd been taken for a ride by an unscrupulous woman who'd read about Damon's death in the newspaper and then claimed to have received a message from her son. Thousands of dollars and untold mental anguish later, Elizabeth had learned that the so-called medium was in fact a con artist wanted by the police.

She glanced at Dr. Summers. "I don't believe all psychics are phonies."

He shrugged. "That's debatable, I suppose."

She hesitated, not sure how much more she wanted to reveal. But it was a little late now to go back. "Some people believe that when a loved one dies, a door is opened. A…gate that connects this world to the hereafter."

"I've heard that theory."

"When I was in a coma after the accident, I think I followed Damon through that gate. I wanted to be with him so badly, but…something kept pulling me back. Dr. Summers…" She moistened suddenly dry lips. "What if when I came back through the gate…someone came with me?"

"This Roland Latimer, you mean."

Elizabeth's hands were trembling, so she kept them hidden beneath the blanket. "What if he's the reason I heard music coming from Damon's room? What if he's the one who scattered toys and slammed doors…because he wanted me to think it was Damon? He wanted to keep me connected to his world any way that he could." She was whispering now, almost afraid to say the words aloud. She was terrified to give free rein to the thoughts and fears she'd been struggling with for months, but she couldn't seem to hold them back. It was as if she'd opened a floodgate.

And it explained so much. Her disconnect from the real world. Her refusal to accept her son's death. Her turning away from the one man who might have been able to help her.

"It's apparent you've given this a lot of thought," Dr. Summers said noncommittally.

Elizabeth closed her eyes. "Believe me, I know how all this must sound to you. But what if it's true? What if this…entity has been using memories of my son to lure me back through that gate? What if it started with the sleeping pills?"

"You think a ghost caused you to take an overdose of sleeping pills?"

"I think my desire to be with my son has made me vulnerable to him. And he knows that. He uses it. He's been waiting all this time for me to come back here, where his hold over me is even stronger…." She trailed off and glanced back out at the mist. "Now do you think I'm crazy?"

"No, of course not. But I do think you're under a tremendous amount of stress." Dr. Summers got up and walked over to the window to stare out. He searched the darkness for so long that Elizabeth had almost started to wonder if he was looking for Roland Latimer.

When he finally turned, his features were set in such a way that she couldn't possibly tell what he was thinking. "Have you told Paul about any of this?"

"No. I wasn't even going to tell you. I was afraid you'd both want to have me committed again. But I know what I saw, Dr. Summers. I know what I *feel*."

"Let me ask you something, Elizabeth. What happens when you see this…entity, as you call him?"

She frowned. "What do you mean?"

"If you truly think he's from beyond, then you must be frightened of him."

"I am."

"What do you do when you see him then? Do you run away?"

Her frown deepened. "No, I can't."

"What do you mean, you can't?"

"I told you, it's like he has some sort of hold on me."

"Do you feel trapped?"

"Yes, but at the same time I'm…drawn to him."

"Would it be fair to say that you experience conflicting emotions where he's concerned?"

She hesitated. "Yes, I guess so."

He walked back over to the bed and sat down. "How did Paul react when you told him you wanted a divorce?"

The question took her by surprise. "We've already discussed that. He agreed to the divorce if I would come up here with him for the weekend."

"It other words, he put conditions on the divorce."

"Yes."

"How did that make you feel?" When she didn't answer, Dr. Summers lifted a brow. "Did you feel trapped, Elizabeth?"

"Yes, I suppose so."

"What about now?"

"I don't know what you mean."

"I think you do. Paul wants to reconcile, doesn't he?"

"He says he does."

"And how do you feel about reconciliation? Conflicted? Torn? Pressured? You see where I'm going with this, don't you?"

"You think Roland Latimer is a symbol of what is going on in my marriage. A manifestation of my emotional state. My confusion." Elizabeth hesitated. "I'm not sure I buy that."

"Is the alternative so much easier to believe?"

"That he's a ghost, you mean?" She shook her head. "I don't know what I believe anymore."

"Which is why I want you to come in for a session next week. We'll talk about all this at length then, but for now you should probably get some rest." He stood. "I'll have my secretary call you and set up an appointment. In the meantime, if you need me for any reason, you know where to find me. And Elizabeth..." He paused at the door. "Try not to worry. We'll get it all sorted out."

Elizabeth wished she could believe that, but whether Roland Latimer was a ghost or a figment of her imagination, there was no way this was going to end well.

Chapter Eleven

Throwing back the blanket, Elizabeth got up and tiptoed to the door. She opened it a crack and glanced out. She couldn't see Paul or Dr. Summers from where she stood, but she could hear them at the front door. They spoke in low tones, and she put her ear to the opening, straining to make out the conversation.

"...stressful time for her. The last thing she needs is to feel pressured," Dr. Summers was saying.

"You gave me that advice once before," Paul said angrily. "And I made the mistake of listening to you then. I gave Elizabeth the time and space you seemed to think she needed and I nearly lost her. I'm not about to let that happen again."

"I understand how you feel, but you have to think of Elizabeth's well-being. She's made great progress in the past several months, but she's still walking an emotional tightrope. If you keep pressuring her, you could push her right over the edge. And this time we might not get her back."

Not wanting to hear any more, Elizabeth slipped away from the door. Undressing, she hung her gown in the closet and put on her pajamas. By the time Paul returned, she'd already climbed back into bed.

"How are you feeling?" He came over to stand at her bedside.

"Much better."

"Do you want something to eat?"

"No, thanks."

"How about some hot tea?"

"I don't want anything, Paul."

"Are you sure?" He glanced around, as if not quite sure what to do or say. His gaze lit on the fireplace. "It's still a little nippy in here. Maybe I should start a fire for you."

"If you want."

He walked over to the fireplace and, kneeling, struck a match to the kindling. Once he had the blaze going, he straightened. "You're all set." He still seemed at a loss. Elizabeth wondered if his reticence had something to do with Dr. Summers's warning. "I should probably let you get some sleep."

When he turned to leave, Elizabeth said quickly, "Paul?"

"Yes?"

She hesitated. "Do you know why I went out to the terrace tonight?"

"You said you were feeling ill."

"I was. But I also saw you with Nina Wilson. You

were both coming back in from the garden, and for a moment I thought…"

His hand dropped from the door and he came back into the room. "Is that what this is all about? How many times do I have to tell you? There is nothing going on between Nina and me."

Elizabeth shrugged. "You keep saying that, but then…I see the two of you together. If there's nothing between you, why doesn't she just go away?"

"I wish I knew," Paul muttered as he walked back over to the fireplace. He adjusted a log, but Elizabeth had a feeling he was just buying himself some time.

When he finally turned, he still had the iron poker in his hand. Firelight flickered over his face, giving him an oddly menacing demeanor. Elizabeth shivered beneath the cover. She couldn't help herself. What if Frankie was right? What if she really didn't know her husband anymore?

"I think she's after something," he finally said.

"Yes, that's obvious."

"I mean money. I think she's trying to set me up for a sexual-harassment suit."

Elizabeth stared at him in shock. "If you really believe that, why did you go outside with her tonight?"

His features tightened in anger as he gripped the fireplace tool. "Because I didn't have a choice. She threatened to go to the police and a file a complaint against you if I didn't hear her out. The woman is trouble, Elizabeth. She's manipulative and devious and she could very well be dangerous. I want you to stay away from her."

The look on his face sent a ripple of alarm up Elizabeth's spine. "What are you going to do?"

"I don't know, but it's not for you to worry about." He replaced the poker and stood with his back to her for a moment.

Elizabeth lay back against the pillows and stared at the ceiling. A premonition descended over her, and she couldn't shake the notion that something bad was about to happen. "Paul?"

He glanced over his shoulder.

"Is there something else going on that I should know about?"

The question seemed to annoy him. "Like what?"

"Frankie told me that you're having problems at work."

His eyes flashed. "And just how the hell would she know that?"

"Is it true?"

He came toward her slowly. "What exactly did she say to you, Elizabeth?"

"She has an acquaintance who works for your firm. That person told her that you lost a lot of money recently when some of your projects fell through. Is it true?"

He looked as if he wanted to deny it, but then he nodded, his expression grim. "I've had some setbacks, but I don't want you worrying about that either."

"But I have a right to know," Elizabeth insisted. "We're still married. We still have joint finances."

He ran a hand through his dark hair. "You're right. When we get home, we'll sit down and I'll go over everything with you. Including my concerns about Frankie."

"Frankie?"

"If you're really worried about finances, Elizabeth, I'd advise you to pay a little closer attention to the shop's accounting practices."

"Meaning?"

"You were away from the business for a long time. Now that you're active again, it might be time to call for an audit."

"You're not accusing Frankie of embezzlement," she said incredulously.

"I'm not accusing her of anything. However, if she's mismanaged the shop's assets, you need to make sure that you can protect yourself." He came back over to the bed and stood looking down at her. "But I don't think we need to get into all that right now either. Like I said, we'll talk about it when we get back to the city. Right now you need to get some rest."

"I'm not tired." Elizabeth wondered if he had purposefully deflected the conversation from his work problems to hers. "And even if I were, I don't think I could sleep. Not with everything you've just told me. I need to know something, Paul. This distrust you have of Frankie…is it sudden or have you always felt this way about her?"

He sat down on the bed. "I've had reservations about her character for some time now, but she's your best friend and business partner. I trusted your judgment."

"What changed?"

"Let's just say my accountant's warnings brought into focus some of the vague concerns I've had about her for years. At the very least, I think she's capable of taking advantage of your trust."

"She thinks you're the one taking advantage of me," Elizabeth said softly.

The anger flared again, so sudden it took Elizabeth's breath away. She'd never thought of Paul as having a temper, but now she couldn't help remembering the flash of rage in his eyes when he'd heard that Nina Wilson had followed her up to the waterfall. And a few minutes earlier, when he'd heard about Frankie's accusations. Obviously the past eighteen months had taken a toll on him, as well. He wasn't the same person either, and Elizabeth suddenly had the feeling that she was staring into the eyes of a stranger.

"How am I taking advantage of you, Elizabeth?"

She tucked a strand of hair behind one ear. "Frankie thinks the only reason you want to reconcile is because a divorce settlement would leave you strapped for cash."

"She actually said that?" A muscle worked in his jaw. "And what do you think?"

"I'm not sure what to think. Sometimes I believe that you still love me. I even start to wonder if divorce is the right answer. And then—"

"You see me with Nina. Or Frankie says something to you."

She nodded.

A shutter came down over his face then. Elizabeth didn't have a clue what he was thinking. "I wish you could trust me."

"I do. It's just…"

He took her hand and laced his fingers through hers. "Maybe I haven't given you reason to trust me. I haven't been completely honest with you, Elizabeth."

"About…Nina?"

He squeezed her hand. "This isn't about Nina. I told you earlier that I took a drive after my meeting with Boyd Carter. That wasn't the whole truth." He paused. "I went into town looking for Roland Latimer."

A tremor of fear shot through her. *"Why?"*

"Because you said he frightened you last night, and I wanted to make sure that he left you alone."

"But you didn't find him, did you?"

Paul's brows lifted in surprise. "How did you know?"

She didn't answer him.

"Have you seen him again?"

She still didn't respond.

"Elizabeth." Paul took her hand in both of his. "He's contacted you again, hasn't he? He said something else to scare you."

She turned her gaze to the swirling fog outside her window. "I don't want to talk about Roland Latimer."

"Why not?"

"Because he isn't real," she whispered.

"I know that."

Her gaze flew to Paul's. "You *know?*"

"I talked to a local historian in town today. She told me that Roland Latimer has been dead for seventy years. He died in the fire that destroyed the original Fernhaven. The man you saw couldn't possibly have been Latimer. Unless he's a ghost." When Paul saw her reaction, he tugged on her hand. "That was a joke."

She remained silent.

"Elizabeth, honey, you can't possibly think the guy you saw is a ghost. It was just someone from town pretending to be this Latimer character. Evidently a couple of the locals have been trying to frighten the staff. He probably saw you on the terrace last night and decided to have some fun. I doubt he's dangerous, but if he keeps bothering you, we'll call the police. Or better yet, I'll take care of him myself."

"No!" She jerked her hand from his.

"Elizabeth…my God, you're shivering. What did he say to you? What the hell did he do?"

Her hand crept to her throat. "You don't understand."

"Understand what? Tell me."

She glanced at the window again. The mist curled and writhed against the glass. She couldn't see Latimer, but she knew that he was out there somewhere.

To get to her, he'd have to get rid of Paul.

The notion occurred to her suddenly, and fear tightened like a fist around Elizabeth's heart. She'd never been so terrified in her life.

ELIZABETH'S REACTION mystified Paul. She couldn't seriously believe that a ghost had approached her on the terrace of the hotel, and yet…it wouldn't be the first time she'd looked for a supernatural answer.

After their son's death, she'd been frantic to find some meaning in the tragedy, and her search had taken her into some pretty dark places. The so-called medium who'd promised her a connection with Damon had been only too happy to take her money and string her along with nebulous messages from the beyond. But Paul thought she'd gotten over all that.

Maybe not. Maybe Julian Summers was right. Maybe Elizabeth was still balanced precariously on that emotional tightrope. One misstep and she could topple over into the dark abyss that had claimed her once before.

And this time we might not get her back.

Paul didn't want to believe it. She seemed so much better to him now. In some ways she appeared stronger than ever. It had taken real courage to pull herself out of that chasm, and he couldn't think that she would allow herself to get sucked back in.

But this business with Roland Latimer…

Somehow he had to find the guy, Paul decided as he paced his room. Bring him face-to-face with Elizabeth and prove to her once and for all that he was just a flesh-and-blood man up to no good. Ghosts didn't exist.

Or maybe what he should do instead was get her away from this place.

Paul walked over to the window and glanced out at

the darkness. He'd had such high hopes that bringing her here would somehow rekindle their relationship. And in some ways it had. Old feelings had begun to resurface. Feelings that Elizabeth could no longer deny.

But there was something strange and oppressive about Fernhaven. He felt it even now. The perpetual mist seemed to wear on his nerves, and Paul found himself anxious to get back to Seattle.

Turning away from the window, he tried to plan out the following day. He had another meeting with Boyd Carter after lunch, and if everything went the way he hoped, he and Elizabeth could be on the road by late afternoon. They could be miles away from Fernhaven by the time darkness fell. By tomorrow night they would be safe and sound in their own home.

What then?

Paul had made her a promise. If she still wanted a divorce when they returned, he wouldn't stand in her way. Was he prepared to keep his word? Despite Dr. Summers's warnings, could he just let her walk away without a fight?

His thoughts growing gloomier by the moment, Paul took a quick shower and climbed into bed. He closed his eyes and tried to will himself into sleep, but it was no use. He was too restless. Throwing off the cover, he swung his legs over the side of the bed, thinking perhaps a walk would help clear his head.

But as he reached for his clothes, a sound from Elizabeth's bedroom stopped him cold. He'd almost convinced himself that he'd imagined it, but then the sound came again, a low, urgent moan. She was having another nightmare.

He strode barefoot and shirtless through the living room. Her door was ajar, and as he pushed it open, a frigid draft struck him across the face like a slap.

Shivering in the cold, he stepped into the room, his gaze going immediately to the bed.

To Elizabeth.

Paul could hardly breathe.

The fire had died down, but the embers cast a faint glow over the room. She lay on top of the covers, her hair fanned against the pillow, her legs splayed as her hands moved intimately over her body.

She was naked, and the sight of her almost stilled Paul's heart. He hadn't seen her that way in months. He'd forgotten how incredibly beautiful she was, slender and lithe, her skin like porcelain.

She groaned again, but not from a nightmare, he realized in shock. She was sexually aroused.

His body reacted instantly to the knowledge, and for the space of a heartbeat he could do nothing but drink in the sight of her. Her head moved restlessly against the pillow as one hand flattened against a breast and the other hand…

The cold brought him sharply back to his senses. It was then that he realized the terrace doors were also ajar. She must have gotten too warm earlier and opened them for some fresh air. But Paul couldn't imagine her leaving them open. Not after their discussion about Roland Latimer.

He hurried over to shut them, making certain once again they were locked. Pulling the drapes across the glass, he turned back to the bed.

Elizabeth lay perfectly still now. He walked over and stood staring down at her, not wanting to cover her and yet knowing he should. It was freezing in her room.

As he reached for the blanket, her hand snaked out and caught his wrist. The strength of her grip took Paul by surprise.

"Don't let him in," she pleaded.

Her voice sent a chill up Paul's spine. "It's okay. It's just me. Everything's fine."

"He won't go away unless…"

"Unless what?" Paul wasn't even certain she was awake. Her eyes were open, but they didn't appear to be focused on him. She didn't sound like herself either. She sounded…

He didn't want to think about how she sounded. How she looked. The way her eyes seemed to glow in the darkness.

"You have to save me from him," she whispered urgently. She rose on her knees then, and as the blanket fell away, Paul drew a ragged breath.

He couldn't tear his gaze from her nakedness. He wanted her at that moment as he'd never wanted her before.

One pale hand slid around the back of his neck and

drew him to her. "Make love to me," she murmured against his lips. "It's the only way…."

She kissed him then with a ferocity that stole his breath. That swept away whatever vestiges of control he'd been trying to cling to.

Falling back against the bed, she pulled him down with her. He lay over her, kissing her desperately as his fingers threaded through her hair.

When they finally broke apart, he tried to rein in his emotions. He'd caught her at a vulnerable moment. He didn't want to take advantage of her.

But the way her body felt against his, the way she looked up at him through hooded eyes…

"Maybe we should slow things down," he murmured.

"No! It has to be now," she said frantically. Her fingers slipped inside his pajama bottoms, searching, finding, stroking.

He groaned. "Elizabeth…"

She tugged at his clothes. Paul peeled them off and kicked them aside. Then he was over her again, his heart pounding against hers.

"I can feel how much you want me," she whispered. "I want you, too." Her hand closed around him, guiding him into her.

Paul wanted to take it slow. They hadn't been together for months. He didn't want to hurt her, but she wouldn't allow him to be gentle. He'd never seen her like this. It was as if…

No, he wouldn't think about that now. He wouldn't

let doubts consume him. Not with Elizabeth naked and aroused beneath him.

Her nails raked down his back, and then she grasped his hips and arched her back, drawing him deeply inside her. She pushed him away, then pulled him back in again and again and again until Paul could no longer fight her frantic rhythm. He gave himself over to her, matching her tempo, holding back only when he felt himself nearing the edge. He didn't want it to end. Not yet…

But even a momentary respite was too much for her. She pushed him off, rolled him onto his back and climbed on top of him. Sliding over him, she stared down at him for the longest moment. Then, throwing back her head, she began to move.

The sight of her that way…hair cascading down her back, breasts gleaming in the dim light, her slender hips moving against his…

Paul exploded inside her. He couldn't hold back. Not one second longer. The climax shook him to his very core, and a moment later, when Elizabeth collapsed, shuddering, on top of him, he wrapped his arms around her and held her as if both their lives depended on it.

Chapter Twelve

When Paul woke up alone the next morning, he wondered for a moment if he'd been dreaming. He was still in Elizabeth's room, in her bed, but somehow it didn't seem possible that they'd spent the night together. There had been times during the long, lonely months of their estrangement when Paul had thought they might never share an intimate moment again.

And in all honesty, he couldn't say that it had ever been quite like *that* for them. Elizabeth had always been passionate, but last night she'd seemed so different.

Like a woman possessed.

The notion made him distinctively uncomfortable, and he tried not to dwell on what Elizabeth's behavior might mean as he sat up in bed and rubbed the back of his neck.

Where was she anyway? And how long had she been gone?

Frowning, Paul called out her name. When she didn't respond, he jumped out of bed and grabbed his pajamas.

Slipping them on, he went through the cottage looking for her. He'd begun to panic a little when he found a note she'd taped to his bathroom mirror. She'd gone up to the waterfall.

Why in the world would she go back up there? he wondered anxiously. After her confrontation with Nina, he thought they'd agreed that she wouldn't go there alone again.

Quickly showering and dressing, he headed out. The overcast sky gave the day a somber look and deepened Paul's anxiety as he followed the trail back into the trees. It had rained during the night. The canopy dripped steadily as strands of mist drifted like gossamer across the path.

The woods all around him were eerily silent. Paul had never been the skittish sort or one prone to a wild imagination. But he found himself glancing over his shoulder now and then, almost expecting to see a wraith-like figure slinking along the trail behind him. A diaphanous form with the face of the man he'd seen in Zoë Lindstrom's book.

Roland Latimer was a very nasty customer. Alive or dead, I wouldn't want to cross paths with him.

As Paul thought back on his conversation with Zoë, he also remembered something Elizabeth had said last night when he'd come into her room and found her naked on the bed. *You have to save me from him,* she'd whispered frantically. And then, *Make love to me. It's the only way.*

Paul had been too caught up in the moment to worry about her motivation, but now he had to wonder what she'd meant by that.

You have to save me from him.

He couldn't get her plea out of his mind, and he found himself glancing over his shoulder once again. For one split second he could have sworn he saw someone standing under one of the trees, and his breath quickened. The man was there one moment, gone the next.

It was nothing, he thought in relief. An optical illusion created by the patchy fog.

He certainly hadn't spotted Roland Latimer lurking in the shadows. The man had been dead for seventy years, and contrary to local legend, Paul refused to believe that Fernhaven was haunted by the spirits of those who had perished in the fire. He'd never believed in the supernatural and he wasn't about to start now.

As he neared the fall, the mist thickened and it was like stepping into another world. A thick, gray, shifting world that seemed to hold time suspended. Over the roar of the water he heard Elizabeth's voice and he wondered who on earth she could be talking to. Hopefully not Nina Wilson. Surely the woman wouldn't have the gall to follow her up here again.

He hurried his steps anyway, and as he emerged from the trees, he heard Elizabeth again. But as he drew within a few feet of her, she fell silent even though she gave no other indication that she was aware of his presence.

She was sitting alone on a log. No one else was around, so she must have been talking to herself.

No big deal. He sometimes muttered to himself at work.

But somehow the sight of Elizabeth sitting alone on that log, staring up into the trees, jarred him more than he cared to admit.

As he followed her gaze, the blood in his veins turned to ice.

Beady eyes stared back at him.

Vultures, he thought in amazement. Through the curls of mist he caught glimpses of their distinctive red heads and hooked beaks. There must have been dozens of them perched in the trees. He'd never seen anything like it. "What the hell—"

"They smell death." Elizabeth's words sent another chill up Paul's spine. He still had no idea if she was addressing him or not, but he chose to believe that she was. Because the alternative was not something he wanted to contemplate.

"They can smell decaying flesh," he corrected. "I don't think they have any particular psychic abilities." Still, he'd never seen so many of them in one place before and he had to admit the sight was a little unnerving.

"I found your note," he said as he came over to sit beside her on the log. "I was a little surprised that you'd come back up here alone."

"I like it up here. There's something special about this place. Can't you feel it?" she said in a hushed, rev-

erent tone. Her face looked beautiful and strangely serene. "It's peaceful, like a chapel."

Peaceful wasn't the word that came to Paul's mind.
Not with the roar from the waterfall and the mist that
seemed to swirl greedily over the rocks.

And vultures gazing down at them from the trees.

But if Elizabeth found it peaceful, even mystical for
some reason, perhaps that explained why she felt so
drawn to the place. Maybe she hadn't been talking to
herself after all, but praying. She'd always been a spiritual person.

"I hope I'm not intruding on your privacy," he said
carefully.

"No, of course not." But in spite of her assurance,
she had yet to meet his gaze. It was as if she couldn't
bring herself to look at him. Was she embarrassed about
last night?

Paul studied her profile. "You're not trying to avoid
me, are you?"

She turned in surprise. "Why would you think that?"

"Because we've been avoiding one another for
months. We've avoided a lot of things, I think. Maybe
we've gone about it in different ways, but we've both
been avoiding life in order to avoid more pain. I don't
want to do that anymore," he said softly. "Not after last
night."

She glanced away. "I don't want to talk about last
night."

"Why not? And don't say it was a mistake," he said

harshly. "Because it wasn't. It was the sanest thing either of us has done in a long damn time."

"I'm not saying it was a mistake."

"Then what?"

She lifted a hand to brush back damp hair. "I'm just not sure it changes anything."

"Maybe not for you," he said, trying to conceal his hurt. "But it changed everything for me. It made me realize how much I've missed our closeness and how badly I've handled things since Damon died. I never should have let you push me away. I never should have let you go through your grief alone."

"I wasn't alone."

He wanted to believe that she was referring to her family and friends, but he wasn't at all sure that was what she meant. She seemed so distant this morning. So…lost.

He reached out suddenly and took her hand. "Let's get out of here, Elizabeth. Let's go back to the cottage, pack up our stuff and get the hell away from this place."

She said, almost in shock, "You want to leave?"

"Why not?" He looked around, trying to suppress a shudder. "This place gives me the creeps," he muttered.

"But…what about your meeting with Boyd Carter this afternoon?"

Paul would have liked nothing better than to blow off that meeting, but he couldn't afford to. Not the way his luck had been running at work lately. "We'll get packed up and leave as soon as the meeting is over. We can be on the road before dark. What do you say?"

But Elizabeth was no longer listening to him. Her attention was caught once again by the vultures in the trees.

"Elizabeth?"

"It's like they're waiting for something," she said in a near whisper.

Paul shrugged. "I expect they're migrating south for the winter."

"I don't think so. I'm afraid…" She broke off on a shiver.

"What, Elizabeth? What are you afraid of?" Something in her voice lifted the hair at the back of Paul's neck.

She put a hand to her throat. "I'm afraid they're waiting for me."

Her words stopped his heart. "Elizabeth, my God, don't talk like that!"

She frowned, her expression perplexed. "I don't—I don't know why I said that."

He grabbed both her arms and turned her toward him. "You're scaring the hell out of me. All this talk about death…" His grasp tightened. "Promise me you'll never try to hurt yourself again."

She gasped in shock. "I would never do that."

"I don't think you would, but…" He pulled her into his arms then and held her as hard as he dared. "I couldn't bear to lose you, too. I couldn't stand it."

As her body trembled against his, he couldn't seem to shake the memory of the day he'd found her unconscious on their bed. She'd been so still and pale and silent, her expression almost serene….

PAUL HAD BEEN RELUCTANT to go off to his meeting once they'd returned to the cottage, but Elizabeth had finally convinced him that she was fine. Although he'd done a good job of hiding it until today, Elizabeth knew he was still haunted by her suicide attempt. She couldn't blame him, of course. She'd tried to kill herself once, and that wasn't something either of them would ever forget.

Still, she knew that no matter what happened, she would never go to that dark place again. It would take some time, but Paul would finally come to realize that, too.

He'd only been gone a few minutes when the phone rang. Thinking that he might have forgotten something, she hurried to pick up. But it was Frankie, not Paul.

"I'm glad I caught you in, Lizzy, because I want to apologize for last night. I'm so sorry for all those things I said. Can you ever forgive me?"

"We both said some harsh things," Elizabeth murmured.

"I know, but I couldn't sleep last night for worrying about how badly I upset you. I'm hoping you'll let me buy you a drink and make it up to you."

Elizabeth glanced at her watch. The afternoon was already slipping away and she still had a lot to do.

"Lizzy? Are you there?"

"Yes, I'm here, but I don't have time for a drink. Paul and I are driving back to Seattle today."

"Oh." Frankie sounded disappointed. "Didn't I see Paul in the lobby a few minutes ago?"

"He has a meeting with some of his investors, but we're leaving as soon as he's finished."

"That could take hours," Frankie said. "You know how those things go. Come on, Lizzy. Surely you can make time for just one drink. I don't want to go another day with all this tension between us."

"I don't know—"

"Wait. Before you say no, I have an even better idea," Frankie said excitedly. "We can't leave Fernhaven without trying the hot springs. That's what this place is famous for! The waters are supposed to be very therapeutic. Almost spiritual, I hear. Have you seen the pools? They're *gorgeous*. We could order a bottle of wine and just relax while Paul's in his meeting."

After Paul had expressed such deep reservations about Frankie the evening before, Elizabeth wasn't at all certain she wanted to spend the afternoon with her. What if Frankie really had mismanaged the shop's assets? Or worse, deliberately embezzled from their capital? Those were matters that would have to be dealt with seriously, and as soon as Elizabeth called for a review of the books, Frankie would know something was up. She'd realize that Elizabeth no longer trusted her, and whatever the outcome of the audit, their friendship, as well as their business relationship, might very well be damaged beyond repair.

But Elizabeth couldn't ignore Paul's warning. Sooner or later she'd have to find out if there was any basis to his concerns. Maybe it was time she started feeling Frankie out about the possibility of an outside examination.

"All right," she finally said. "But I can't stay long."

"You can leave whenever you want," Frankie said eagerly. "I'm just glad you're coming. I'll meet you at the pools in ten minutes."

Elizabeth hung up slowly, hoping she'd done the right thing. Before she could change her mind, she hurried over to her half-packed suitcase to dig out her swimsuit.

A few minutes later she joined Frankie at the pools. They had the whole area to themselves. The threat of rain and the cooler temperatures must have chased everyone else inside, Elizabeth decided as they disrobed and slipped neck-deep into the steamy water.

The place was wonderfully secluded and serene. Mist covered the lush underbrush like a soft blanket, while vapor from the heated pools curled upward through the tall trees, disappearing against a gray sky.

It was a strange, mystical place, and after a few moments Elizabeth began to relax. She felt more at peace than she had in days. The minerals in the water really did seem to have restorative qualities.

Frankie gave a long, contented sigh. "I could stay here forever. This place is heaven."

"You'd get bored sooner or later." Elizabeth sat down on a ledge and reclined against the wall of the pool.

"You're probably right. But it's a great way to spend a cloudy afternoon, you have to admit. I'm glad you came, Lizzy."

"It is nice," Elizabeth murmured.

"Do you know what I was thinking about before I called you?" Frankie asked softly. "I was thinking about the first time we met. It had to be—what—ten years ago. You and Paul had just moved to Seattle."

"Of course I remember." Elizabeth tilted her head back and gazed at the hazy sky. "I'd been beating the pavement for days. I saw your shop and was intrigued by the name, so I decided to walk in and ask for a job."

"That's right. God, it seems like yesterday, doesn't it? I even remember what you had on—that terrible green dress you'd made for yourself." Frankie gave a wry chuckle. "Who knew that lurking beneath that shapeless sack was such a talented designer? I took one look at that chartreuse menace and almost dismissed you on the spot. Then I saw your sketches and was completely blown away. I knew you could help me put Frankie Loves Johnny on the map, but I couldn't afford to hire another designer."

"So you offered me a partnership."

"Smartest thing I ever did," Frankie said. "Your talent and my marketing savvy—we're a hard team to beat, Lizzy."

It was the opening Elizabeth had been looking for. She knew she should mention the discrepancies in the financial statements Paul had told her about, but she couldn't seem to bring herself to do it. Not now, not in this place. There would be plenty of time for that once they got back to Seattle.

So she closed her eyes and said nothing as the water lapped at her chin.

"Can I make a little confession?" Frankie said after a moment.

Apprehension fluttered along Elizabeth's backbone. "What is it?"

"I used to be a little jealous of you. Even though I realized I needed your help to make a go of the shop, a part of me resented the fact that I couldn't do it on my own."

"But that's not true," Elizabeth said. "You're a talented designer in your own right. You were successful long before I came along."

"There's success…and there's success," Frankie said with a shrug. "I'm a realist. I don't have your training or your natural talent. But that's okay because I have other strengths. Your designs may have put us on the map, but I'm the one who's kept us there. Especially these past eighteen months."

Who was she really trying to convince? Elizabeth wondered uneasily. Why did she have the unpleasant notion that Frankie was setting her up for something? That this whole afternoon, including Frankie's apology, had been a subtle manipulation? "I know I haven't been pulling my weight, but that's going to change," Elizabeth told her.

"Then you've decided not to sell your partnership?" Frankie asked anxiously.

"I haven't made any decisions yet. But if and when I do decide to sell, we may need to get an independent appraisal to establish fair market value. That could mean a full audit of the books. You wouldn't have a problem with that, would you?"

Frankie shrugged. "Why would I?" But in spite of her nonchalant response, she sounded a bit defensive.

"I just wanted to mention it," Elizabeth said carefully. "If an audit becomes necessary, I wouldn't want you to think that I'm going behind your back."

"I've always appreciated your honesty, Elizabeth."

Elizabeth—not Lizzy all of a sudden. A wedge had already been inserted into their relationship, and Elizabeth knew that the chasm would probably grow wider in the coming weeks. She didn't want to believe it, but she suddenly had a strong suspicion that Paul could be right. Frankie was hiding something from her.

"Could I ask you something?" Frankie asked with a frown.

"Of course."

"Does Paul have something to do with your sudden desire for an audit?"

"I told you why an audit might be necessary. If I decide to sell—"

"I know what you said, but I have a feeling there's more to it. What has he said to you?"

"Paul has nothing to do with this," Elizabeth insisted.

"Who are you kidding?" Frankie said bitterly. "Everything you do involves Paul."

Elizabeth shot her a surprised look. "What do you mean by that?"

"You're never going to divorce him no matter what he does. We both know that."

"Frankie—"

"Oh, I know. I sound like a bitter old maid, don't I? Well, guess what? That's what I am."

Elizabeth stared at her in astonishment. She'd never heard Frankie talk this way before. "You're a beautiful woman, Frankie, and you're barely forty years old. You could have any man you wanted, but you've never shown the slightest interest in settling down. So what's brought all this on now?"

"I don't know. Biological clock and all that, I guess. Or maybe sometimes I just think it would be nice to have someone look at me the way I've seen Paul look at you."

"But you've never wanted a serious relationship. I've heard you say it a dozen times."

"I still don't. Didn't. It's just…lately I've started to wonder…." Frankie trailed off and glanced at Elizabeth. "I actually was in love once. Does that surprise you?"

It did a little. "Anyone I know?"

"No." She plowed her fingers through the water. "We met in college, like you and Paul."

"What happened?"

She shrugged. "It didn't work out. We wanted different things out of life, so we went our separate ways. We still keep in touch, though. Christmas cards, the occasional phone call."

"Does he live in Seattle?"

She gave Elizabeth a sly look. "I didn't say it was a he, now did I?"

Elizabeth tried to hide her shock. "No, I just assumed…"

Frankie laughed. "I'm teasing you. His name is Nathan Grandholme. He's an attorney in Portland. Last I heard, he and his wife are expecting their third child. Three kids…" She shuddered. "Can you imagine?"

Elizabeth said nothing.

"Oh, Lizzy, I'm sorry," Frankie said in horror. "God, that was thoughtless of me. I was only referring to my own lack of maternal instincts. I didn't stop to think…"

"It's okay," Elizabeth said quietly. "You don't have to keep walking on eggshells around me."

"I know that." Frankie sighed. "And anyway, this conversation is getting way too maudlin. You know what we need?" she said with forced brightness. "That drink I promised you. How about some wine?" She climbed out of the pool and reached for her robe.

"No, wait," Elizabeth said. "I can't stay much longer."

Frankie glanced over her shoulder as she slipped on the robe and belted it around her waist. "Just one drink, Lizzy. Come on. For old times' sake."

"All right, just one," Elizabeth relented. "But make it quick, okay? I really do have to get back to the cottage and finish packing."

"I'll be back in a flash."

Frankie gave a quick wave over her shoulder as she disappeared down the path toward the hotel.

Elizabeth sank back into the water and closed her eyes. The peacefulness of the place was lost on her now. The conversation with Frankie had left her oddly unsettled. She would never have guessed that her friend was envious of her relationship with Paul. Frankie didn't even *like* Paul. Or at least, that was certainly the way it seemed lately. She'd gone out of her way to make Elizabeth aware of her husband's alleged transgressions, and now Elizabeth suddenly had to wonder about Frankie's motives.

"Elizabeth…"

Her whispered name sent a chill spiraling through her. Elizabeth's heart started to pound as she sat up in the water and glanced around.

No one was there.

"Elizabeth…" The whisper came again and again, hanging on the mist like an echo.

"Elizabeth…"

Scrambling out of the pool, she grabbed her robe and wrapped it tightly around her. She couldn't see him yet, but she knew he was there, hiding in the mist. Waiting, watching…

"Elizabeth…"

Her heart hammered against her chest as she turned to follow Frankie up the path to the hotel. But a movement in the pool caught her eye, and everything inside her stilled.

She didn't want to look, but she couldn't help herself. Stepping near the edge, she glanced down. She could see nothing through the thick cloud of steam, but she heard a faint sound, a ripple, as if someone had skipped a stone across the surface.

And then the vapor melted away, and Elizabeth found herself staring into crystal clear water. There was something just below the surface. She couldn't quite see…

It was a child, she realized in horror.

A child underneath the surface of the water.

Chapter Thirteen

The boy appeared to be standing on the bottom of the pool, reaching up to her. He had dark hair, dark eyes and pale, translucent skin.

He wasn't real. Elizabeth knew that. He couldn't be real. Her son was dead. She couldn't be seeing him...and yet he was there, just below the surface of the water.

She blinked.

He was still there.

He opened his mouth and bubbles floated to the surface.

Elizabeth screamed as she fell to her knees and plunged her hands into the water. "Oh, my God..."

She tried to grab his hand, but as she leaned forward, she lost her balance and tumbled into the water. Her head hit the rocky ledge, and her skull exploded with pain. She must have blacked out for a split second, because when she came to her senses, she was lying on the bottom of the pool.

A scream rushed to her throat as she tried to stand

up. The sash of her robe had somehow gotten wrapped around her throat and become tangled beneath the ledge.

Terror sliced like a razor through Elizabeth as she tore at the belt. When she couldn't get it loose, she tried to slip out of the robe, but the fabric was like a dead weight, holding her just beneath the surface.

She struggled for what seemed an eternity, but no matter how hard she fought, she couldn't free herself. Her muscles weakened as her lungs screamed in agony.

After a moment the pain went away and a feeling of well-being came over her. She closed her eyes, succumbing to the lethargy that tugged at her consciousness.

She heard her name called as if from a great distance, and then someone grabbed her arms and yanked her to the surface.

The moment the cold mist hit her face, Elizabeth sputtered and gulped in air as her rescuer hauled her out of the water. They both collapsed on the soggy ground, Elizabeth on her back and Frankie on her knees, hovering over her.

"Lizzy…are you all right?" she gasped.

Elizabeth rolled to her side and coughed up water. After a moment, when she finally had her lungs cleared, she tried to sit up.

Frankie had her hand over her mouth, watching her. "Oh, God, oh, God, oh, God," she kept whispering.

"I'm okay," Elizabeth finally managed as she massaged her throat.

Frankie closed her eyes, as if to say a quick prayer. "What happened? When I saw you under the water like that, I thought…oh, God, never mind what I thought. I'm just glad you're okay—"

"Did you see him?" Elizabeth bolted upright and glanced around. "Did you?"

Frankie still seemed to be in shock. Strands of dark hair were plastered to the side of her face, and she was shivering uncontrollably. "See who? Who are you talking about?"

Now it was Elizabeth who started to tremble. "He was here, Frankie. He kept calling my name. He made me think Damon was in the water and then he trapped me. He tried to kill me."

"*Damon?* Oh, Lizzy, no…" Frankie placed her hands on Elizabeth's shoulders. "Listen to me. There was no one here with you. Do you hear me? You were alone. You must have fallen and hit your head. I think we need to get you to a doctor."

Elizabeth clung to her. "I don't need a doctor. I need…Paul. I want to see Paul."

Something flashed in Frankie's eyes. "Okay, just calm down. I'll find him for you. But first let's get you back to the cottage. We'll both freeze to death if we don't get out of these wet clothes."

A FEW MINUTES LATER they were back at the cottage. Elizabeth found a dry robe for Frankie and then went back into her room to change while Frankie made tea.

"Careful, it's hot," she warned as she handed Elizabeth a cup. They both sat down on the couch.

"Did you call Paul?" Elizabeth asked anxiously. A knock sounded on the door at that moment, and she let out a breath of relief. "That must be him. He probably forgot his key."

Frankie set aside her cup and went to let him in. The murmur of low voices drifted back from the doorway before Frankie finally reappeared with Dr. Summers.

Elizabeth stared at her therapist in surprise. "What are you doing here?"

"I called him," Frankie confessed. "I thought you needed to see…a doctor."

"A psychiatrist, you mean," Elizabeth said with a frown.

"I'm also an M.D.," Dr. Summers reminded her. "Frankie said you fell at one of the pools and hit your head. Maybe I'd better have a look." He came over and sat down beside Elizabeth on the couch.

"I'm fine," she insisted. "It's not my head I'm worried about."

"I'd still like to take a look anyway." He probed the back of her head gently. "Hmm, there's a bump all right. I doubt it's anything too serious, but you could have a mild concussion. Have you experienced any dizziness or disorientation?"

"No."

"Yes," Frankie corrected her. Her gaze collided with Elizabeth's. "I'm sorry, Lizzy, but you were extremely disoriented when I pulled you out of the pool." She paused and bit her lip. "She thought someone tried to kill her."

Dr. Summers studied Elizabeth. "Is that true?"

She sighed. "What's the point of telling you what really happened when you aren't going to believe a word I say?"

Dr. Summers turned to Frankie. "Could you give us a moment?"

She gave Elizabeth a worried glance. "Sure. As long as you're going to be with her. I'll go back to my room and change. But if you need me, you know where to find me." She hesitated for another moment, then turned and walked out of the room.

When they heard the door close behind her, Dr. Summers said softly, "So why don't you tell me what happened?" When Elizabeth didn't respond, he gave her a prompt. "Who do you think tried to kill you?"

She closed her eyes briefly. "Roland Latimer. The man I told you about last night."

"The ghost, you mean."

She nodded.

"Why do you think he wanted to kill you?"

She answered automatically. "So that we can be together."

"Ah." Dr. Summers thought about that for a moment.

Elizabeth flashed him an angry look. "What's the diagnosis? Are you ready to call the men in white coats to come and take me back to the psych ward?"

"I don't think that'll be necessary," he said with a smile. "It's possible that what you're experiencing is a reoccurrence of post-traumatic stress disorder brought on by your decision to divorce Paul. Nightmares, feelings of estrangement and detachment, even hallucinations are all classic symptoms of PTSD."

"I know that. I've gone through all that before, remember? It's different this time."

"How?"

Before she could respond, the door opened and Paul walked in. His gaze went from Elizabeth to Dr. Summers, then back to Elizabeth. "What's going on?"

Dr. Summers stood. "Elizabeth is fine now, but she had an accident earlier."

"An accident? Are you all right?" Paul said in consternation. "What happened?"

"Didn't Frankie call you?" she asked with a frown.

"I haven't talked to Frankie since last night." He hurried over and sat down beside her. "Are you sure you're okay? What happened?"

When Elizabeth hesitated, he glanced up at Dr. Summers. "For God's sake, would someone please tell me what's going on here?"

"Elizabeth fell at one of the pools and hit her head. Frankie found her underneath the water."

Shock registered on Paul's face. "Underneath…oh, my God."

Elizabeth turned. "It's not what you think. I didn't… it wasn't on purpose, I swear."

Paul took her hand and squeezed it, but his face had gone deathly pale. "What were you doing at the pools? I thought you were going to spend the afternoon packing."

"I was. But Frankie called and wanted to meet, and I thought it would be a good opportunity to sound her out about an audit. When she left to get us a drink, I…slipped and fell. She called Dr. Summers because she thought I needed medical attention."

"She has a bump on the back of her head," Dr. Summers confirmed. "But as I told her earlier, I don't think it's anything to worry about. However, I recommend that she rest quietly for the next several hours. It's possible she could have a mild concussion."

"Shouldn't we get her to a hospital?" Paul said worriedly.

"I don't think a hospital visit is necessary," Dr. Summers said. "Just keep a close eye on her for the rest of the day. If she experiences any dizziness or disorientation or if you have a hard time waking her, then take her in as quickly as possible. There's a clinic in the nearest town, I believe. Or you can always call my room. I'm not checking out until tomorrow."

"We were planning on driving back to Seattle this afternoon," Paul said.

Dr. Summers frowned. "I wouldn't advise it. If Elizabeth were to experience problems on the road, you could be miles away from the nearest medical facility. At least here you'll have the clinic nearby."

"I suppose another day won't matter," Paul murmured.

Dr. Summers glanced down at Elizabeth. "You'll call my office when you do get back to the city?"

She nodded.

"Good. I'll leave you two alone for now, but if you need me for any reason, don't hesitate to call." He started for the door. "Paul, a word, please?"

Paul got up and walked him to the door.

Elizabeth could hear them talking, but she couldn't make out their conversation. She had a feeling, though, that Dr. Summers was filling Paul in on everything she'd told him.

When he came back into the room, his expression was troubled. "Can I get you anything? More tea?"

"No, I'm fine."

"Are you in pain? Do you need an aspirin?"

Her chin trembled as she gazed up at him. "All I need is for someone to believe me."

He came back over to the couch and sat down beside her. "I want to believe you, Elizabeth." He took her hand. "You have to know that."

"But you can't."

He gave a helpless shrug. "I don't believe in ghosts. I'm sorry. There has to be a logical explanation for all this. I still say someone is trying to frighten you."

"Not someone. Roland Latimer. And he's trying to do more than frighten me." She clutched Paul's hand. "He was there. I heard him. And before you say anything, I know he's dead. He died seventy years ago in the fire. But I also know what I saw. I know what I heard. I know what I *feel*."

Paul sighed. "Okay. Just tell me everything that happened. Maybe if we go over it enough, we can start to make sense of it."

She nodded. "After Frankie left, I heard him calling to me. He kept whispering my name. And then I saw Damon in the water."

Paul flinched.

Elizabeth put trembling fingertips to her mouth. "He was reaching up to me, Paul. I knew he wasn't real, but I had to touch him. I had to make sure. Can you understand that?"

Paul glanced away. "Yes," he said hoarsely.

"I tried to take his hand, but I fell into the pool. I guess I must have blacked out for a moment, because when I came to, the belt of my robe was around my throat. He'd trapped me beneath the water."

Pain flashed across Paul's face. "It couldn't have been Damon. Even if it were somehow possible for him to come back, he would never hurt you. He adored you."

Elizabeth's eyes filled with tears. "I know that. I know it wasn't him. It was Roland Latimer. He's somehow using Damon to…stay connected to me."

"Elizabeth, my God, think about what you're saying," Paul said harshly.

She jerked her hand from his and stood. "I know how all this sounds, Paul. Roland Latimer is dead and ghosts don't exit. I know all that. But he was there. He was in the pool with me. He was in my room last night and the night before. I can't always see him, but I know he's always there. And he won't rest until…"

Paul rose slowly. "Until what, Elizabeth?"

"Until I'm dead, too," she whispered.

ELIZABETH BARELY TOUCHED her dinner that night, and even though she knew she wouldn't be able to sleep, she decided to turn in early. She dug a book out of her suitcase and settled down in bed, preparing to spend a long, restless night.

Paul came to her door to say good-night. "I'll stretch out on the couch," he said uneasily. "That way, if you need anything, all you have to do is call out." He walked over and checked the lock on the French doors, then pulled the drapes closed.

"Paul?"

He turned.

Elizabeth closed her book and laid it aside. "About what I said earlier...I know you don't believe me. I can't blame you for that. But I want you to know that...I'm not going off the deep end again. It's different this time. I don't know what's happening to me, but I'm not crazy."

He came over to her bedside, his face tense as he stood staring down at her. "I don't think you're crazy, Elizabeth. I can't pretend to understand any of this...." He shrugged helplessly. "I'm not predisposed to look for a supernatural answer. That's not the way I'm wired. But I have to admit there's something about this place that's getting to me, too. I'm wondering now if we should have left earlier, as we planned."

"It wouldn't make any difference," she told him softly.

He frowned. "What do you mean?"

"It's not this place that's haunted. It's…me."

"Don't talk like that." Paul took her hand and drew it to his lips. "Everything will be okay once we get back to Seattle. You'll see."

"I wish I could believe you." She couldn't seem to stop trembling. "I'm scared, Paul. Not just for me but for you. I think the only way he can get to me is if…he somehow keeps us apart. I'm terrified of what he might do."

"Then we'll just have to stay together, won't we?" Paul sat down on the bed. "We're getting the hell out of here first thing in the morning. I'm not letting you out of my sight until we're miles away from this place. I'll even sit over there in that chair until the sun comes up."

"You don't have to do that."

"I want to."

"No, I mean…" Elizabeth hesitated. "You don't have to sleep in the chair or on the couch just to be near me."

He threaded his fingers through hers. "I'd do anything for you. Don't you know that by now?"

A lump rose in her throat. "I think I'm finally beginning to." She scooted over in bed and turned back the covers. "What I meant was…the couch is probably not all that comfortable. And I know that chair isn't. After last night, it seems silly that we can't share the same bed."

Something flared in his eyes. Without another word he reached over and turned off the light. Undressing quickly, he slipped under the covers and drew her to him, nestling her in the curve of his body.

They still didn't talk. The silence continued for so long that Elizabeth thought he must have fallen asleep. She moved ever so slightly and his thumb grazed her breast. Desire darted through her, and she marveled that so slight a touch from him could still affect her so deeply.

Pressing herself against him, she placed her hand over his and lifted it to her breast. His body reacted instantly, and he groaned into her ear, "Are you sure about this?"

She nodded.

Letting her head fall back against his shoulder, she lifted her lips to his. He kissed her gently at first and then with growing heat as she opened her mouth and tangled her tongue with his.

He held her close as one hand moved down her stomach and slid between her legs. Elizabeth shivered. He knew just how to touch her. Soft, soft strokes that deepened as the pressure inside her began to build.

She gasped and pushed his hand away. "Not yet," she whispered desperately.

He knew exactly what she wanted. Shifting their bodies slightly, he slid into her, rocking against her as his fingers found her again.

Their lovemaking wasn't as fierce or as desperate as the night before, but somehow it was more profound this time. More intimate and healing.

Elizabeth wanted the moment to last forever, but she couldn't hold on. Her body went rigid and Paul's arms tightened around, holding her close as they climaxed together.

"I love you," he murmured into her ear. He said it over and over, and Elizabeth thrilled to the knowledge.

After everything they'd been through, after everything she'd done to push him away, he still loved her.

She suddenly wanted to weep at all the wasted months. "I love you, too," she whispered.

At that moment, in Paul's arms, she felt safer than she had in a long, long time.

PAUL CAME AWAKE SLOWLY. He wasn't sure what had roused him, but he knew instinctively something wasn't right. He had an odd stinging sensation at the side of his neck.

He lifted his hand to the inflamed area and winced. His skin was hot to the touch and very tender. He had no idea what had happened to him. He'd been fine earlier.

He noticed something else, too. The temperature had dropped in the room. He sat up and glanced around.

The French doors were ajar, and he swore. He knew damn well he'd closed and locked them earlier.

Had Elizabeth gotten up sometime during the night and opened them?

He glanced down at her. She appeared to be sound asleep. When he saw her breath frosting, the hair at the back of his neck lifted. For the first time since all the talk about ghosts had started, Paul experienced real fear.

The cold inside the room was unnatural somehow. Damp and fetid. He could almost feel the evil.

Climbing out of bed, he went over and closed the French doors. He turned the lock, then shoved a chair beneath the latch. He wasn't sure why he bothered. If they were dealing with something supernatural…

He tried to laugh off his apprehension. This place really was getting to him.

Going into the bathroom, he closed the door and turned on the light. Tilting his head back, he glanced in the mirror. "What the hell—"

Angry red streaks radiated down the side of his neck to just beneath his chin. The wounds were raw and beaded with blood…like fresh claw marks.

His heart thudding, he grabbed a bottle of Elizabeth's astringent and doused his neck, cursing at the sharp sting.

Something was very wrong here. Something he didn't understand. Something he didn't even believe in.

Look for a logical explanation, he chided himself.

Maybe Elizabeth had scratched him during their lovemaking. He remembered her nails raking down his back the night before, but the marks she'd left had been nothing like this.

Patting his neck dry, he went back into the bedroom and checked the door. It was still closed and locked, and the temperature had already warmed.

As he climbed back into bed, Elizabeth roused and rolled over. "Paul?"

"I'm still here," he said softly. "Everything's okay."

"Are you sure?"

"Yes. Go back to sleep."

She closed her eyes and drifted off.

Paul propped his pillow against the headboard and settled back, prepared to spend the rest of the night with his eyes wide open.

Chapter Fourteen

Paul's eyes flew open. He'd only meant to close them for a moment, but he must have drifted off sometime after dawn.

Squinting at the bedside clock, he swore. He'd been asleep for hours. It was almost noon, but the sky was so overcast, the gray light filtering in through the windows hadn't awakened him.

Swinging his legs over the side of the bed, he sat for a moment, his hand going to his neck. The marks were still there. He hadn't dreamed them after all.

Elizabeth must have scratched him in her sleep. Or maybe he'd scratched himself. In the light of day, the supernatural explanations he'd entertained earlier seemed even more far-fetched. There was a logical reason for everything that had happened at Fernhaven. There had to be.

Even so, Paul was suddenly prodded by an urgency to get the hell out of there. He and Elizabeth should have been on the road hours ago.

And speaking of Elizabeth…where was she?

The urgency dogged him as he got up and searched the cottage. It was like a repeat of the day before, except this time she hadn't left a note.

Dressing quickly in black slacks and a turtleneck sweater to hide the scratches, Paul headed back up to the waterfall. When he emerged from the trees this time, though, Elizabeth was nowhere to be seen.

He called her name, softly at first and then with a cold growing dread. Where *was* she?

That same dread drew him to the edge of the cliff. As he stood gazing down at the crashing water, Paul's heart catapulted to his throat. Something was down there….

Oh, God…

Panic mushroomed inside him as he scrambled down the slippery rocks, clinging at times to nothing more than his fear as his feet slipped out from under him. Finally he jumped down to the wet ground, then splashed through the frigid pool at the bottom of the waterfall.

The woman lay facedown in the water.

Dear God, no!

A mind-numbing terror seized him a split second before he realized it wasn't Elizabeth.

His heart still thudding, Paul drew the dead woman onto the bank and rolled her over. Threads of red hair clung to her face as lifeless green eyes stared up at him.

It was Nina Wilson.

Shock rolled through Paul, and with it a wave of

nausea. He took a moment to steady his nerves, then he reached for her wrist to check for a pulse even though he knew she was gone. Her skin was bluish-white and cold. She'd been dead for a while, he thought.

And then he noticed something else. The open eyes and gaping mouth. Whatever she'd seen before she died had terrified her. A scream had been trapped on her face.

Shaken, Paul stared down at her wondering what had happened. The fall had frightened her, of course. She must have gotten too close to the edge and slipped.

Or been pushed.

Slowly he lifted his gaze to the top of the cliff as a dark suspicion came over him. For a moment he could have sworn someone stood at the edge gazing down at him.

The image faded quickly, and he was left with Nina's warning ringing in his ears…

Elizabeth isn't the person you think she is. She's not just troubled. She's seriously demented. She even tried to kill me this afternoon. Did she tell you that?

ELIZABETH HAD JUST finished packing when she heard Paul let himself into the cottage. "I'm in here," she called out. A moment later he appeared in the bedroom doorway, and she glanced up in relief. "I was beginning to worry.…" Her words trailed off when she saw his expression. "What's wrong? Paul…your clothes are all wet. What happened?"

He came over to the bed where she stood in front of her suitcase. "Where were you this morning?"

The suspicion in his tone took her by surprise. "Frankie called. We met for coffee."

"Why didn't you wake me?"

"You looked so peaceful. I thought you needed some rest before we started back."

"But we agreed to leave first thing this morning," he said accusingly.

"We can leave now." Elizabeth closed her suitcase. "I'm almost ready."

But he couldn't seem to let it go. "Why didn't you tell me where you were going, Elizabeth? You could have at least left a note. You didn't think I'd worry?"

"I guess I thought I'd be back before you woke up. I'm sorry. I didn't mean to upset you." She came over to the side of the bed and put her hand on his arm. "What's this all about anyway?"

He gave her a look she couldn't quite decipher. "Maybe I'm having a little trouble figuring you out. Last night you were terrified to be left alone, but this morning you had no problem going off to meet Frankie without my knowing."

"I'm sorry," she said again. "I should have told you where I was going. Frankie and I still had some things to settle, and I was anxious to get it over with. As it turns out, you were right about her. She hasn't been up front with me about some of the things she's done at the shop. She admitted that we've lost money. I don't know how bad it is yet, but she's agreed to a full audit when we get back to Seattle."

"So…you were with Frankie all morning?"

She gave him a puzzled look. "Paul, why all the questions? What's got into you?"

"What's got into *me?*" He turned away, putting a hand to the side of his neck. "Last night you were convinced that you're being haunted by a man who died seventy years ago. You even thought he tried to kill you. And now today…you're acting as if nothing happened."

She sat down on the bed. "I'm still frightened. It terrifies me to think about what happened at the pool yesterday. But I've been going over and over it in my head, trying to make sense of it. Maybe Dr. Summers is right. He thinks what I'm experiencing is symptomatic of PTSD."

Paul lifted a brow. "You're coming to that conclusion now? Why?"

"Because ghosts don't exist." She drew a shaky breath. "It's not possible for someone to come back from the dead. You said it yourself. There has to be a logical explanation for everything that's happened."

"Maybe I was a little hasty in my conclusion," he muttered.

"What?"

He sat down beside her. "Elizabeth…did you go up to the waterfall earlier, before you met Frankie?"

"No, why?"

"You seem drawn to that place for some reason. I thought you might have wanted to go back up there before we left."

"I didn't go up there, Paul. Not this morning."

He nodded and glanced away. "There's something I have to tell you. It's about Nina Wilson."

Elizabeth's heart skipped a bit. "What about her?"

He paused. "She's dead, Elizabeth."

Her hand flew to her throat. "Oh, my God. How? When?"

"I found her at the bottom of the waterfall a little while ago. She must have fallen from the cliff."

Elizabeth gasped. "*You* found her?"

"I went up there looking for you."

Was it her imagination or had the accusing note crept back into his voice? "Paul, you can't think…"

Something flickered in his eyes.

She stared at him in shock. "You think I pushed her, don't you?"

"Of course not," he answered too quickly.

"It wasn't me," Elizabeth whispered. "I swear—"

He grabbed her hand. "I know it wasn't you. It was probably an accident. She slipped on the wet rocks. I'm sure the police will come to the same conclusion, but in the meantime they've asked me to come with them to the county sheriff's office to give a statement."

"They're taking you in?" Elizabeth asked fearfully.

"I'm not under arrest, if that's what you mean. But I am considered a material witness since I'm the one who found the body. And because Nina worked for me. I'm the reason she came up here in the first place."

He was also the one who had a motive for wanting

to get rid of her, Elizabeth realized suddenly as snippets of their previous conversations came back to her.

I don't want you worrying about Nina Wilson. I'll take care of her.

Elizabeth's gaze lifted to Paul's and she started to tremble. "What are you going to tell them?"

"I guess it depends on what they ask me," he evaded.

"Paul, if they find out that she was in love with you, that she was trying to make trouble for us…"

His gaze darkened. "You don't need to worry about this. I'll take care of it."

"But I am worried. Don't you see?" Elizabeth clutched his hand. "It's him. Latimer. He made this happen. He's using Nina's death to keep us apart—"

"For God's sake, stop talking about Roland Latimer," Paul said harshly.

"Why? Because the police might think I'm crazy enough to kill someone?"

"Elizabeth—"

"I know how it sounds, Paul." She brushed a strand of hair from her face with a trembling hand. "But what if it's true?" she whispered. "What if he really is trying to keep us apart? You can't leave me here alone. I have to come with you."

"That's not a good idea." He stood abruptly. "I don't want you talking to the police."

"But I don't have anything to hide," she protested. "I didn't kill Nina."

"We know that, but the police may not see it that way.

Look, I'll get everything cleared up and then we'll be on our way. Just stay inside and keep the doors locked until I get back. Let me handle this my way, Elizabeth. I don't want you involved."

Elizabeth rose, too. "I'm already involved. If the police find out that Nina accused me of trying to push her off that same cliff, they'll want to talk to me. You can't stop them."

"They're not going to find out," he said flatly.

"But you can't withhold information from the police!"

He placed his hands on her shoulders. "Just calm down, okay? Let me take care of this. Call Frankie to come over and stay with you until I get back." Fishing his keys out of his pocket, he tossed them on the bed. "I'm leaving the car here with you just in case."

"Just in case what?" Elizabeth asked, worried. "You are coming back this afternoon, right? We're still going home today."

"Yes, of course. We'll hit the road as soon as I get back. I just don't want to leave you stranded here while I'm gone." The edge in his voice made Elizabeth shiver. He was worried, too, no matter what he said to the contrary. Why else would he insist on leaving the car if he was that certain he'd be coming back today?

But surely the police wouldn't arrest him. They had no evidence. Did they?

He turned toward the door, but Elizabeth caught his hand. "Paul—"

He swept her into his arms then and held her close.

"Try not to worry. Everything's going to be fine. But right now I have to change out of these wet clothes. They're waiting for me."

She nodded and let him go, taking a few moments to collect herself before she followed him into the other bedroom. He'd already changed into a pair of jeans and now he sat shirtless on the edge of the bed as he pulled on dry socks and shoes. When he heard her at the doorway, he glanced up. "Can you grab me a shirt—"

Elizabeth gasped when she saw the marks on his neck. "Oh, my God, Paul. Who did that to you?"

His hand flew to his neck as his gaze met hers. Something that might have been guilt flashed in his eyes.

ELIZABETH STOOD AT THE bedroom window watching the rain that had begun to fall shortly after Paul left. He'd been gone for hours, and she'd nervously watched the time tick away as darkness had crept over the pouring sky, obliterating the last of the light until nothing could be seen beyond the terrace.

Inside the cottage all was silent, except for the steady drum on the rooftop. There was a dank smell in the air, as if the rain had somehow seeped through the windows and doors. The scent had come suddenly with the early twilight, followed by a bone-chilling cold. Thunder cracked in the distance, the roar echoing through the cottage for one split second before everything fell silent again.

Rubbing her arms briskly to alleviate the cold, Elizabeth watched the rain. She'd long since finished packing and now all she could do was wait. She'd tried to call the police station a number of times, but had never been able to get through to Paul. She hadn't been able to reach Frankie either, and the feeling of isolation she'd been battling all afternoon threatened to engulf her now. And with the loneliness came fear. Elizabeth's thoughts turned to the scratches on the side of Paul's neck.

He didn't know how he'd gotten them, he'd told her earlier. He'd awakened in the middle of the night to a strange stinging sensation. Somehow the marks had appeared on his skin while he'd slept.

How was that possible? Scratches didn't just…appear. And yet the alternative was no less unthinkable.

I don't want you worrying about Nina Wilson. I'll take care of her.

Squeezing her eyes closed, Elizabeth forced away the image of Paul and Nina Wilson standing on that cliff. She wouldn't think about that. She couldn't. It was too incredible. Paul wasn't a violent man. He would never hurt another person, no matter what.

Elizabeth believed him about the scratches because she'd seen and heard too many things herself that couldn't be explained. But what would the police think if they saw those marks? The same thing that had crossed her mind when she'd first seen them?

Thunder crackled again, and Elizabeth jumped when the lights flickered. Panic skittered along her backbone. The last thing she needed was for the electricity to go off.

She busied herself finding candles and matches just in case. Lighting the long tapers, she shook out the match, then went back to her vigil at the window.

A draft of frigid air pushed through the glass. Glancing down, she saw that the French door had come open a crack. It had been closed when she'd gone to find the candles. Closed and locked. She was sure of it.

The room was getting colder by the moment. Elizabeth tried to shut the door, but the wind whipped it back.

Her heart pounding, she grabbed the door and forced it closed. Turning the bolt, she glanced through the glass. Something was on the terrace. A cloud of mist that remained untouched by the rain. The vapor hung right outside her door, as if waiting for her to open it and let him come in.

She screamed when the phone rang, her heart thrashing against her chest like a wounded bird. Realizing that it might be Paul, she rushed to answer.

"Hello?"

"Elizabeth?"

"Paul." She closed her eyes in relief. "Where are you? Are you on your way back?"

He sighed wearily. "No, not yet. Is everything okay there?"

Elizabeth's gaze shot to the French doors. She could no longer see the mist, and the room seemed to have gotten warmer. Maybe he'd gone away....

Her hand crept to her throat. "I need you to come back, Paul. *Now.*"

"I'm trying my damnedest. But there was some kind of emergency. A multiple-vehicle collision on one of the highways. They're shorthanded around here, so I'm stuck at the police station until someone gets back to give me a lift."

"Maybe I should come get you," Elizabeth said nervously.

"I don't know if that's such a good idea. The weather is really getting bad out there."

Elizabeth cast another glance toward the window. "I have to get out of here, Paul. It's already dark, and I can't...I can't bear the thought of spending another night in this place."

"I don't want that either." He hesitated. "Is Frankie there with you?"

"No. I called her room earlier, but she didn't answer. Maybe she's already checked out."

"Damn it, I don't want you there alone," Paul muttered. "All right, come pick me up. But promise you'll be careful."

She closed her eyes in relief. "I will."

"Do you know how to get here?"

He gave her directions, and after they hung up, Elizabeth blew out the candles, then grabbed her raincoat and car keys. She almost expected to find her way blocked by that strange mist when she opened the front door, but the trail was clear.

Dashing out into the rain, she tried not to look back as she splashed along the path to the shimmering lights of the hotel, almost sobbing in relief when she spotted the valet standing beneath the portiere.

He held an umbrella for her while another brought around the car.

"Take it easy out there," he warned as Elizabeth slid behind the wheel. "These mountain roads get treacherous in weather like this."

"I will."

She pulled away from the hotel, and as she made the turn onto the main highway, a weight seemed to lift from her heart. Glancing in the rearview mirror, she could see the lights of Fernhaven receding in the distance and she let out a shaky breath. At that moment she couldn't imagine ever going back. She'd pick up Paul and they would just keep driving. They could have their luggage shipped to them in Seattle.

She almost laughed with relief. *I'm free,* she thought. *I got away.*

The rain started coming down harder, and she reached for the windshield-wiper control. But the blades started up automatically, and the radio came on, blasting static so loudly that Elizabeth jumped, almost losing control of the car. She tried frantically to turn off the volume, but the knob spun uselessly in her hand.

In between crackles of static she could hear strands of music, something soft and delicate. Elizabeth went cold inside. It was a lullaby, the one she used to sing to Damon when he was a baby. The one she still heard playing in his room when she was alone in the condo.

She began to sense that she wasn't alone in the car and she let out a sobbing breath.

"Damon," she whispered.

She could feel him beside her even though she knew he wasn't there. If she turned her head, the seat would be empty. She *knew* that. So she wouldn't take her eyes off the road the way she had that day eighteen months ago. She *wouldn't*. Not even for a split second.

His scent rose all around her as the lullaby tugged at her memories. His laughter drifted up from somewhere deep inside her heart.

Mom, look what I made you!

The exact words he'd said to her that day.

Dear God, how could she resist?

Elizabeth glanced at the empty seat beside her. No one was there, of course. She'd only imagined Damon's voice. Her son was dead. He wasn't coming back to her….

Blinking back tears, she forced her attention back to the road. Someone was standing on the pavement directly in her path.

A man dressed all in black.

Roland Latimer.

His gaze seemed to burn into Elizabeth's as he put up a hand to stop her.

She tried to swerve, but the car struck him head-on. She felt no impact. It was as if he'd somehow gone right through the metal.

Screaming, Elizabeth hit the brakes, and the tires skidded on the wet pavement. The steering wheel spun in her hands as the car careened out of control and plunged down an embankment, plowing over rocks and slamming with a bone-jarring rattle into a tree.

Chapter Fifteen

Frankie rushed toward Paul as he came through the glass doors of the tiny clinic in Cedar Cove. "Thank God you checked your messages," she said breathlessly. "When I couldn't find you at the cottage, I didn't know what else to do but call your cell phone—"

"Where is she?" Paul cut in. "Is she all right?"

"She's pretty banged up, but the doctor says she'll be fine in a day or two."

Paul closed his eyes in relief. When he'd heard Frankie's message earlier, he'd been almost paralyzed with fear. Memories had assailed him. Another accident. Damon dead and Elizabeth in a coma fighting for her life...

It had been the worst day of Paul's life. He would never forget that first terrible moment when he'd learned of his son's death. The numbing disbelief followed by the horror. The agonizing pain in his chest that had threatened to overpower him. He still sometimes dreamed about that moment.

And then seeing Elizabeth so still and silent in that hospital bed…

The knowledge that she was clinging to life by a thread was the only thing that had kept him going during those first few days. He'd had to remain strong for her. He'd sat at her bedside day and night, willing her to fight her way back to him.

That same helplessness tore at him now as he grabbed Frankie's shoulders. "Where is she? I have to see her."

"I'll take you to her. Her room is just down the hall."

Paul followed Frankie down the corridor and into a tiny cubicle barely large enough to hold one bed. The moment he spotted Elizabeth, his chest tightened so painfully he could hardly breathe. Her eyes were closed, and she looked so fragile with all those bruises on her face—

"She's not unconscious," Frankie rushed to assure him. "The doctor gave her a sedative. She's just resting."

Paul went over and stood beside her. He picked up her hand and held it to his cheek.

Her eyes fluttered open. "Paul…"

"I'm here. Everything's okay."

She clutched his hand. "I saw him again. I didn't imagine him. He was *there*…."

"Where, Elizabeth?"

She drew a ragged breath. "He walked in front of my car. He tried to stop me from leaving. When I swerved—"

"Shush, don't talk. Just rest."

"Don't you see?" she whispered desperately. "He's not going to let me leave here."

A terrible dread settled over Paul. He was suddenly terrified—for Elizabeth and for himself. She was right, he thought. Even if they did leave this place, he was never going to get her back. She was lost to him, and she had been ever since their son died.

He stood at her bedside holding her hand until she finally fell back asleep. Pulling the covers up around her, he turned and walked over to where Frankie stood at the window watching the rain.

"What happened?"

Frankie shook her head. "Evidently she lost control of the car on the wet pavement. Luckily another vehicle was behind her and the driver called 911."

"How did you find out about it? I thought you'd already checked out."

"I decided to wait until the weather cleared up. I was hanging out in the lobby and I overheard someone talking about the accident. When they mentioned the make of the car, I had a terrible feeling it might be Elizabeth. And then when I couldn't reach either of you…" She drew a shuddering breath. "I found out where they'd taken her and I got here as fast as I could. Paul, where was she going all alone like that? Did you two have a fight?"

He frowned. "Why would you think that?"

Something glinted in Frankie's eyes. "I heard about Nina Wilson. It's all over the hotel. There's even speculation that she was murdered."

Paul shrugged. "There's no evidence of that. The police believe it was an accident. She had too much to drink and slipped."

"Is that really what they think?"

Paul's scowl deepened at her tone. "What are you getting at?"

"Were you having an affair with her?" Frankie blurted. "Was that the reason Elizabeth was leaving without you?"

"There was nothing between Nina and me," Paul said angrily. "Elizabeth knows that. She wasn't running away from me. She was coming to pick me up."

Frankie stared at him for a moment, then turned away. "I wish I could believe that," she muttered.

"I'm not the one who's been lying to her, Frankie."

She whirled back to him, her expression outraged. "I've been completely forthright with Elizabeth! She knows everything."

"Don't play the innocent," Paul said coldly. "You only came clean when you were cornered. I've suspected for a long time that you've been playing fast and loose with the books, but I'm only now starting to put it all together. What I can't figure out, though, is how you knew anything about *my* work. Who told you about my projects falling through? Was it Nina?"

She started to deny it, but then her chin lifted defiantly. "What if it was?"

"Then you admit you knew her?"

Frankie hesitated. "I knew her slightly. She used to

come into the shop occasionally while Elizabeth was still out."

"I think you knew her a little better than that," Paul accused. "In fact, I think you may be the reason she came up here this weekend."

"That's ridiculous," Frankie scoffed. "She came up here to be with you."

"She'd have no reason to think we'd be together unless someone encouraged her. The two of you cooked up a scheme to break up our marriage, but I haven't quite figured out why."

Frankie looked stricken. "It wasn't like that! You make it sound as if I was deliberately trying to hurt Lizzy, and I would never do that. She's my best friend, for God's sake. I was trying to *protect* her."

"Protect her from what?"

Frankie's eyes flared. "From *you*."

"Elizabeth doesn't need protecting from me."

Frankie's chin came up again. "That wasn't the way it seemed to me. Not after I talked to Nina."

"Then maybe you'd better tell me how the two of you hooked up," Paul demanded.

Frankie ran a hand through her hair in distress. "Like I said, she used to come into the shop. We started talking. When I found out she worked for your firm, I mentioned that I knew you. I could tell by her reaction that something was wrong, so I finally got her to admit that you and she were having an affair."

"That was a lie," Paul said in disgust.

Frankie's expression tightened. "She was very convincing."

"I'm sure she was." He took a moment to get his anger under control. "You told her about us, didn't you? You related some things about our marriage that Elizabeth had confided in you. Did it never occur to you that Nina might have had an ulterior motive for pumping you for information about us?"

Frankie frowned. "What do you mean?"

"I think she was setting up a sexual-harassment suit against me. I suspect she's done that sort of thing before. And you played right into her hands."

Frankie's gaze faltered. "How do I know you're telling me the truth?"

"Because I've got no reason to lie. Admit it, Frankie. It suited your purpose to have Elizabeth believe the worst of me. Anything that would make her less inclined to believe the worst of *you,* right?"

"It wasn't like that," Frankie insisted. "It wasn't that…calculating. I believed Nina about the affair because I could see how it might happen. You turning to another woman, I mean. You and Elizabeth had been estranged for months. When she told me that she wanted a divorce, I knew how torn up she was about it. I thought that if she found out about you and Nina, it might make things easier for her."

"So you arranged for that to happen, didn't you?" Paul said bitterly. "The day the two of you saw us at the restaurant—that was your doing."

Frankie nodded. "I knew you and Nina were going to be there. I didn't have the heart to tell Elizabeth straight out about the affair, and even if I had, I'm not sure she would have believed me. She had to see for herself."

Paul glared at her. "Have you told the police any of this?"

Frankie's eyes widened in shock. "The *police?* Why would I talk to the police about this?"

"Right now they tend to believe that Nina's death was an accident, but if they decide to reevaluate the case, your relationship with her could make you a suspect."

Frankie gasped. "A suspect? But I didn't kill her! I swear it." Almost inadvertently her gaze darted to Elizabeth.

"Don't say it," Paul warned.

"But...if she thought you were having an affair with Nina—"

"She didn't, in spite of your best efforts."

Frankie didn't look convinced. "Are you sure? You and I both know she's been acting very strange lately. Hearing voices. Seeing things that aren't there. You heard what she just said about someone not letting her leave here. My God, Paul." She put a hand to her mouth. "And then yesterday at the pool...if you could have seen the look on her face. She almost had me convinced. I even thought for a moment..."

"What?"

Frankie bit her lip. "When I tried to pull her out of the pool, it was as if someone really was holding her down."

Paul's heart quickened. "She said her belt was caught beneath a ledge."

"I yanked the belt free, but I still couldn't get her up. I know this sounds crazy, but…" Frankie's voice trembled. "For a moment I thought I saw someone in the water with her. A man…"

Paul grabbed her arms. "Why didn't you say something before now?"

"Because it couldn't have been real! He couldn't have been there one moment and gone the next. He couldn't have vanished like that unless…" She trailed off on a shudder.

Unless he was a ghost.

The chill inside Paul deepened as he remembered all the strange things that had happened since they'd arrived at Fernhaven. The unnatural cold inside Elizabeth's bedroom, the accident at the pool, the scratches that had appeared on his neck after they'd made love…

Don't you see? He's not going to let me leave here.

His grip tightened on Frankie's arms. "I have to go out. There's someone I need to talk to, but you have to promise me you won't leave Elizabeth alone. Not even for a second."

Frankie's eyes widened in alarm. "I won't, but Paul…what I just said…you can't possibly think—"

"I don't know what I think," he said grimly. "Just stay with Elizabeth until I get back. Whatever you do, *don't leave her alone.*"

"I'VE ALWAYS BELIEVED that some men are born with evil inside them." A book lay open on Zoë Lindstrom's knees as a cup of tea cooled on the table in front of her. Firelight flickered in her silver hair, making it appear to glow from certain angles. She looked almost angelic, seated on her sofa talking about ghosts, and as Paul watched her, a shiver slid up his spine.

"Go on," he said as he left the fireplace where he'd been standing and came over to sit beside her.

"Roland Latimer was such a man. Cruel and cunning from childhood." She closed the book and set it aside, as if she could no longer bear to look at his picture. "He was from a wealthy aristocratic family back east, and for years they were able to use their money and power to bury his crimes. Shortly after his twenty-first birthday, however, a girl he'd been seeing went missing. Her family had money and connections, as well, and when they started making inquiries, Latimer's family shipped him off to Europe. He remained there for nearly twenty years, until his father died. Then he returned to Boston to take control of the family fortune.

"Soon after he returned, he met another woman, one much younger than he. Like a true sociopath, he could be quite charming and charismatic when the need arose. He swept the young woman off her feet, but even before the wedding she began to experience his cruelty. She tried to call off the marriage, but it was too late. The two families had already merged their businesses, and she was persuaded to continue with the arrangement."

"What happened to her?" Paul asked softly.

"Somehow she managed to gather her courage and run away from Latimer on their wedding night. One can only imagine what must have happened," Zoë said with a shudder. "He followed her to Fernhaven, where she'd gone to meet her childhood sweetheart. The day after the fire, her body was found floating in the pool at the bottom of the waterfall."

Paul stared at her in shock. He had a sudden image of Nina Wilson lying facedown in the same pool. "Latimer killed her?"

Zoë sighed. "We'll never know for sure, of course, but the police concluded that she'd been strangled before she went over the cliff. It's always been my belief that Latimer killed the poor thing in cold blood, then went back up to the hotel to celebrate. When the fire broke out, he was trapped in the ballroom along with the others. One might easily think of that night as a divine intervention if not for all those innocent lives that were also lost." When she reached for her tea, Paul noticed that her hands weren't quite steady.

"Even if everything you say is true, even if I could somehow accept that Latimer has come back from the dead," he said doubtfully, "why Elizabeth? What does he want with her?"

Zoë took a delicate sip of her tea, then set aside her cup. "Perhaps he sensed her vulnerability. Perhaps your wife, as I do, has the ability to see and hear things that others can't, and that's why Latimer is so drawn to her. For whatever reason, he formed a connection with her and now he won't rest until he has what he wants."

Fear iced through Paul's veins. "He wants her dead."

Zoë nodded, her eyes darkening as she gazed at Paul. "That's the only way they can be together."

"But if I take her back to Seattle—"

"He would follow. His hold over Elizabeth is stronger here, but it isn't Fernhaven that keeps him connected to her. It's your son."

"How?"

"The bond between your wife and son is powerful. So strong that it couldn't be severed even in death. Latimer uses that bond to keep Elizabeth tied to his world."

"Damon…" Paul closed his eyes briefly. "Is he…"

"He isn't with Latimer," Zoë said quickly. "It's his memory that Latimer uses. It's your wife's reluctance to let him go. Your son is safe, Paul. Latimer can't touch him."

"How can you know that?" he asked hoarsely.

"I can't explain how I can know these things." She gave him a comforting smile. "It isn't for me to question. All I can tell you is that your son is able to communicate his happiness to me. When I think of him, I see the brightest of lights. I feel warmth all around me." She put her hand on Paul's arm.

He wanted to snatch it away. He didn't want to believe anything Zoë was telling him, and yet…what choice did he have? He'd seen things with his own eyes that defied explanation.

Paul could feel Zoë's fingers through his sweater, and the hair lifted at the back of his neck. He had the strangest feeling that something had entered his body, and the urge to pull away, to severe the connection, was irresistible at first.

And then he felt it…the warmth and the light and the joy that she had spoken of. It was like nothing he'd ever experienced before. He couldn't explain what was happening to him, but he no longer wanted to turn away. Instead he wanted to cling to that moment forever.

Memories swept over him, some that had come back to him every single day since his son had died and some he hadn't thought of in years. He and Damon playing catch in the park. Fishing together in a crystal clear stream. Baseball games, birthday parties, nighttime stories told under a canopy of stars. The images were all there, stored safely in his heart.

He heard a voice, not in his ear but somewhere deep inside him.

Love you, Dad.

I love you, too, son.

When the warmth started to fade, Paul wanted to weep.

Zoë removed her hand from his arm, but her blue eyes still shone with that strange light. "Your son is safe. He'll always be safe and happy. You don't have to worry about him anymore. Your wife is the one who still needs you."

Paul wiped away the moisture from his face. "How do I stop him?"

"You can't stop Latimer. His power resides within your wife. To break his hold, the bond between her and Damon must be severed. She has to let him go. Once that connection is broken, Latimer's power will diminish."

Paul found that his legs were trembling when he stood. "I have to get back to her."

"Yes. Don't leave her alone. Especially not tonight."

"Why tonight?" Paul said urgently.

Zoë ignored his question as she glanced past him to the door. "How did you get here earlier? I didn't hear a car."

"I ran from the clinic."

"All that way? Here—" she pressed a set of keys into his hand "—take my car. It'll be faster. I have a terrible feeling.…" She trailed off as a clap of thunder sounded in the distance. Her gaze lifted to Paul's and he saw that the light in her eyes had been replaced by a dark, knowing fear. "I have a terrible feeling that time is of the essence," she whispered.

WHEN ELIZABETH OPENED her eyes, she had the strangest feeling that she was trapped in a recurring nightmare. Waking up in a hospital room, Frankie dozing at her bedside…she'd had this dream before.

But where was Paul? Shouldn't he be here? she thought with a flicker of panic. Holding her hand and coaxing her back from that dark place through which she'd once entered so willingly.

Why was the room so cold? she wondered suddenly. It felt like a grave….

And then she saw it. A cloudlike form that hung suspended at the end of her bed. Elizabeth gasped, her heart catching for a moment before slamming painfully against her rib cage.

"Frankie!" she whispered frantically. "Frankie, wake up!"

But Frankie kept right on sleeping as the cloud shimmered and thickened.

Terrified, Elizabeth rose up on her elbows and watched as the vapor took on substance. Suddenly the mist was gone and in its place was a child. A boy. The son she'd thought lost to her forever.

Elizabeth put a trembling hand to her mouth.

The dark eyes, that sweet face…

She squeezed her eyes closed. "You're not real," she said aloud.

But when she opened her eyes, he was still there, the slightest hint of mischief flickering across his features. He lifted a hand and beckoned to her.

A movement behind him caught Elizabeth's eye, and she saw something then that she hadn't noticed before. Someone else was in the room with them. A shadowy form hovered just behind Damon, and as Elizabeth watched in horror, a skeletal hand lifted to the child's shoulder.

"No!" she whispered and rose up out of bed. "I won't let you have him."

IGNORING THE WARNING stare from the nurse at the front desk, Paul raced down the hallway and burst into Elizabeth's room. He paused in the doorway, his heart pounding against his chest.

The bed was empty.

Frankie was sound asleep in a chair, her head thrown back, softly snoring. She didn't even rouse when Paul hurried inside to check the bathroom. Coming back out, he knelt in front of her chair and grabbed her shoulders. "Frankie, wake up. Where's Elizabeth? Where did she go?"

"What?" she murmured drowsily.

His grasp tightened on her shoulders and he gave her a shake. "Wake up!"

Frankie's eye flew open and she glanced around. "Paul...what happened?"

"You fell asleep," he said accusingly. "Where's Elizabeth?"

"Elizabeth?" Frankie glanced at the bed, then her eyes widened. "She was here a minute ago, Paul. I swear it. I only closed my eyes for a second."

"You didn't see her leave?"

"Of course not! I would have stopped her."

He rose and paced for a moment, then spun back to her. "Where are your car keys?"

"My car keys—" They noticed her handbag at the same time. It was lying on the floor, the contents scattered around it.

Frankie bent and rummaged through the items, then upended the purse. "My keys are missing," she said desperately. "Elizabeth must have taken them. Oh, my God, Paul…where do you suppose she's gone off to?"

Paul didn't answer. He was already headed toward the door.

A FEW MINUTES LATER, he pulled up in front of the hotel and leaped out, not bothering with the ticket the valet tried to thrust at him. Racing up the trail to the cottage, he unlocked the front door and hurried inside.

"Elizabeth!"

The cottage was dark and so silent he could hear nothing but the sound of his own heartbeat drumming in his ears. He tried the light switch, but the electricity appeared to be off.

"Elizabeth, are you here?"

Still no answer, but a light flickered in the bedroom and a strange scent lingered in the air. It smelled faintly of lilacs and…dust. Not unpleasant exactly, but one that lifted the hair at the back of Paul's neck just the same. He made his way through the darkened cottage to Elizabeth's bedroom.

Pausing on the threshold, he glanced inside. The flickering light he'd seen from the other room was candlelight, he realized. Elizabeth must have just been here. Maybe she'd stepped out for a moment.

He started toward the open French doors, then came

to a dead stop. Something barred his way. A frosted vapor just inside the door that hung motionless in the air.

As Paul watched, the mist thickened and gradually took on a human shape. Standing before him suddenly was a young woman of about twenty with flowing dark hair and alabaster skin. She wore an old-fashioned ball gown in shimmering white silk, and diamonds glittered in her hair and around her throat.

She gazed at Paul for a moment as if she knew him, and a look of quiet urgency gleamed in her eyes. Turning to glance over her shoulder at the darkness beyond the open doorway, she seemed to stiffen, as if seeing something outside that alarmed her. When she turned back to Paul, her delicate features had contorted in fear. She opened her mouth, but the scream was silent, eternal….

It came to Paul then who she was. Latimer's young wife. The woman he'd strangled and whose body he'd thrown from the waterfall.

She had come here to warn Paul. He didn't know how he knew that, but somehow he did.

The room suddenly grew frigid, and with the cold came the smell of decaying flesh. As if something dead had come in with the wind.

Paul shivered in the unnatural cold, his gaze locked onto the young woman. From the corner of his eye he saw something just outside the door, a gathering mist that thickened menacingly as it moved inside and swirled toward the young woman. Suddenly alarmed, Paul took a step toward her, but she shook her head as if to warn him away.

The cloud swept toward her, and as it touched her, she began to evaporate as if being swallowed up by the darker, stronger vapor.

Someone whispered in his ear, "She's mine," and a chill shot through Paul's bloodstream. The voice seemed to reach inside his chest and squeeze his heart so tightly he couldn't breathe for a moment. He was frightened for the young woman and he was frightened for himself. But mostly he was frightened for Elizabeth.

The putrid smell grew stronger as the cold deepened, and the French door slammed shut with such force that the glass rattled in the panes. Outside the bedroom another door slammed and then one by one the locks began to turn.

"She's mine," the voice whispered over and over. "She's mine, she's mine, she's mine."

Paul started toward the French door, but something knocked him back. He stumbled, righted himself and lunged for the door again. This time he was slammed back with such pressure that his body crumpled against the fireplace. He crashed to the floor, his head colliding with the brick hearth, and after an explosion of pain, everything went black.

ELIZABETH STOOD AT THE top of the roaring waterfall, gazing across the slippery rocks to the other side. She could just make out Damon's form against the backdrop of trees.

It's not him, a little voice whispered inside her.

It was a trick of the mist or perhaps her imagination. It wasn't Damon.

But it didn't seem to matter because Elizabeth couldn't turn away from his image. One way or another, she had to get to him. She had to protect him, save him as she hadn't been able to that day in the car.

Someone was with him on the other side. That same dark shadow hovered just behind him.

"I won't let you have him," she whispered, then more loudly said, "Do you hear me? You can't have him!"

Latimer's taunting laugh came to her over the roar of the waterfall. And then he reached out and took Damon's hand, drawing him deeper into the darkness.

When Paul came to, the lights in the cottage were blazing. He blinked at the sudden brilliance, then lifted a hand to touch the pain at the back of his head. His fingers were bloody when he brought them away, and for a moment he had no idea what had happened.

Elizabeth had left the hospital and he'd come back here to find her. Something had happened…he couldn't quite remember….

His gaze lit on the French doors across the room. They stood open, and an icy breeze blew through, helping to revive him.

Paul staggered to his feet, taking a moment to regain his equilibrium before he started toward the doors. As he stepped outside, he heard the distant roar of the waterfall and he suddenly knew where Elizabeth had gone.

Still groggy, he rushed along the damp path, as dread gathered inside him like a storm cloud. When he emerged from the trees, Elizabeth was nowhere to be seen. He stood at the edge of the cliff and called her name. Wind whipped at his clothes as he peered into the darkness. He could see nothing below him but swirling mist and crashing water.

And then a sound, like a whisper, drew his attention upward, and something caught his eye at the top of the waterfall. As he watched, the mist cleared and he saw Elizabeth on the slippery rocks twenty feet above him.

He wanted to call out to her again, to warn her, but he didn't want to startle her. His heart pounding in fear, Paul started up the treacherous rocks.

ELIZABETH TOOK A tentative step onto the rocks. Her foot slid, and for a moment she wavered precariously on the brink before regaining her balance. Steadying her nerves, she took another step and then another. She was halfway across before she stopped to glance up.

She could see nothing but mist on the other side, but she knew that Latimer was there waiting for her. And so was Damon.

She took another step and faltered when she heard her name. She thought at first it was Latimer calling to her, or even Damon. But then she realized the sound had come from behind her. She glanced over her shoulder and saw Paul on the rocks, moving toward her.

"Paul, don't!" she shouted. "I have to do this."

"No, you don't." He inched his way toward her. "Just stay where you are. I'll come get you."

"You don't understand!" she cried. "He's got Damon!"

"No, he doesn't," Paul shouted over the wind and the crashing water. "Damon is safe, Elizabeth. Latimer can't touch him."

"I saw *him*. Don't you see? I saw him with Damon. I have to stop him. It's the only way." She started to turn away, but Paul's voice drew her back.

"Elizabeth, look at me!"

She turned slowly to face him.

He reached out his hand to her. "Take my hand. Everything will be okay, I promise. I won't let anything happen to you. Just take my hand."

"Damon—"

"He's gone, Elizabeth, but I'm still here and I love you. I've always loved you. Just take my hand."

"I can't."

"Yes, you can. It's okay to let him go. It's what he wants."

"How can you know that?" she cried.

"Because he told me."

His words sent a tremor through Elizabeth. She wanted to believe him. She wanted to take his hand and let him lead her to safety, but...how could she turn her back on her son? He was there in the mist with Latimer.

"Do you love me, Elizabeth?"

She drew a shaky breath. "Yes. More than anything."

"Then trust me. Take my hand and it'll all be over."

She let out a sobbing breath and reached for Paul's hand. As their fingers touched, a gust of wind swept over her, almost knocking her over the edge. Her feet slipped on the rocks, and she screamed, her arms flailing wildly as she toppled toward the brink. Then Paul's hand closed around her wrist and he drew her back.

"Just hold on tight," he shouted. "You're safe now."

They inched their way across the rocks, and the gale grew in strength, whipping at their linked hands as if trying to tear them apart. Paul's grasp on her tightened. "Don't stop," he shouted. "Just keep going."

The moment Elizabeth stepped off the rocks, the wind began to howl, an eerie, enraged sound that might have come from Latimer himself.

She buried her face in Paul's shoulder, trying to block out that terrible sound, as his arms came around her and held her close. "You're safe. He can't touch you now."

She lifted her head as the sound finally abated. "Is he gone?"

"Yes. There's no one here but you and me."

She started to glance back at the waterfall, but Paul gently turned her away. "Don't look back," he said.

"Damon—"

"He's not there, Elizabeth. He was never there. But he'll always be here." He put his hand over her heart. "No one can ever take him away from us."

With trembling fingers he wiped away her tears and then his own.

Elizabeth placed her hands on either side of his face. "I love you," she whispered.

"Keep saying that," he said fiercely. "Don't stop until we're miles away from this place."

As he brushed his lips against hers, the weight that had clung to her heart for so long melted away, and in its place was a glimmer of hope.

"Let's go home," Paul said after a moment.

The hotel arranged a rental car, and they drove late into the night. Eventually Elizabeth fell asleep, her head resting on Paul's shoulder. They were safely away from Fernhaven, but he didn't draw an easy breath until he saw the lights of Seattle glimmering on the horizon.

Perhaps in a couple of days he and Elizabeth would go in to see Dr. Summers and talk out everything that had happened. And in the next few weeks business problems would have to be dealt with, plans made for their future, but those were matters to be decided at some later point.

Right now the city beckoned.

With a steady hand Paul guided them home.